Vanished

Philip Antony

Illustrated by

Annette Cummings

Copyright © 2025 by Philip Antony

All rights reserved.

No portion of this book may be reproduced in any form without written permission from the publisher or author, except as permitted by U.S. copyright law.

To all the kids, big and small, for their patience and support throughout this project. Philip, Elisa, Camilla, Jennifer and Erica, Sara and Kim – this is for you. You helped breathe life into Tommy and the other cast of characters. Thank you.

Philip.

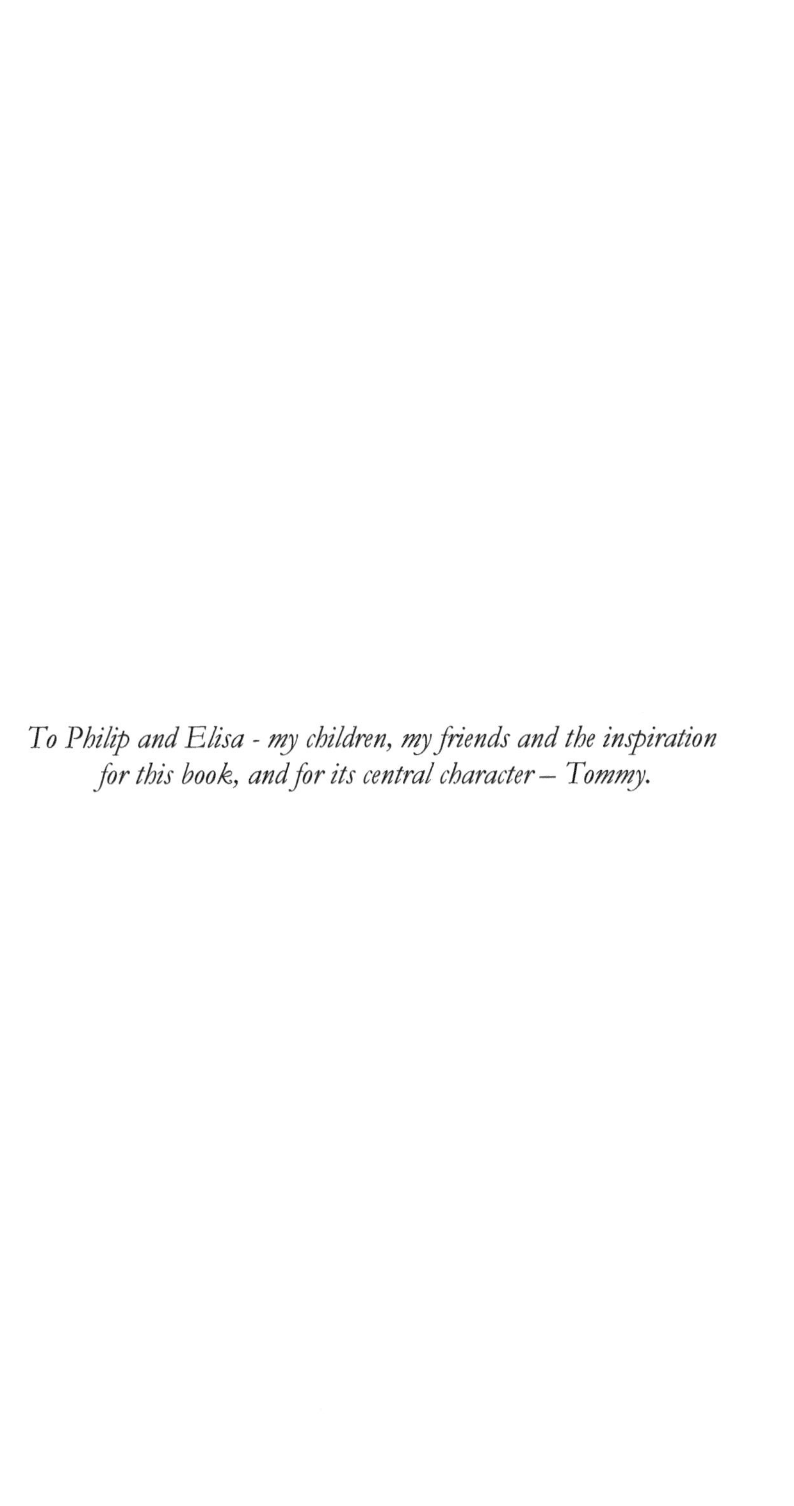

To Philip and Elisa - my children, my friends and the inspiration for this book, and for its central character – Tommy.

They're not Out There, *they're already here . . .*

ACKNOWLEDGEMENT

Books are not easy write. It took me several years to write this one. I must have started and stopped a dozen times. I got frustrated and walked away from it. I banged on the keys, paced the floor, and in the end, even started talking to myself. And when it was all over, I looked around and discovered the strangest thing: I really hadn't written this book alone. These were the generous souls who had sat with me for endless hours drinking coffee and listening patiently into the night as I spun my fantastic journey. They read each chapter, made notes and offered gentle suggestions, most of which have been woven into my tale. To these brave and patient friends, I offer my heartfelt gratitude.

One of the most difficult tasks in writing a book falls to the person who edits the manuscript and turns it into a final work product. In this case, the editor who "volunteered" to edit the book was Sara Jean - my partner, friend and wife. Editors by nature must be cruel and gentle; detailed but able to see the whole story; and possess an endless supply of patience to plow through page after page looking for the errant coma or misspelling – of which she possesses an unlimited supply. This book would never have seen the light of day were it not for Sara Jean's dedication, patience and generosity.

Another special thanks to my friend, Annette Cummings, for lending her talent as an artist to illustrate "Vanished." She captured the people, the places and events; and in so doing, brought Tommy and all my characters to life.

However, I must reserve my special thanks to the kids who read the manuscript before I felt brave enough to send it to the publisher. These kids offered the keenest insight, and the most helpful suggestions to improve the story. Such insightful margin notes as: "This is stupid"; or "Nobody talks that way"; or "Cool" were the guideposts to keep the story readable and believable for my audience. Like sculptors with clay, they helped me to fashion the characters into real people, and to come alive with real words and feelings. To my young friends: Jennifer, Mary Patricia, Kayleigh, Pamela, Kim, Camilla, Melissa and Stephen, you did a really cool thing. Thank you.

Philip Antony.

TABLE OF CONTENTS

CHAPTER 1 1

CHAPTER 2 7

CHAPTER 3 12

CHAPTER 4 14

CHAPTER 5 20

CHAPTER 6 23

CHAPTER 7 28

CHAPTER 8 32

CHAPTER 9 37

CHAPTER 10 49

CHAPTER 11 56

CHAPTER 12 61

CHAPTER 13 66

CHAPTER 14 72

CHAPTER 15 78

CHAPTER 16 81

CHAPTER 17 88

CHAPTER 18 90

CHAPTER 19 100

CHAPTER 20 104

CHAPTER 21 111

CHAPTER 22 112

CHAPTER 23 120

CHAPTER 24 121

CHAPTER 25 129

CHAPTER 26 136

CHAPTER 27 138

CHAPTER 28 146

CHAPTER 29 153

CHAPTER 30 157

CHAPTER 31 160

CHAPTER 32 163

CHAPTER 33 178

CHAPTER 34 181

CHAPTER 35 193

EPILOGUE 232

PROLOGUE

His name is Tommy Flagg. He's ten years old and lives in the Midwest of the United States in a farming community named Ellenville. He loves baseball, especially pitching, and is convinced that he will be the Most Valuable Player in the 2026 World Series.

At the time, Tommy was attending school in the nearby community of Pine Creek....

CHAPTER 1

It was one of those mornings when you wished it was Saturday and you could pull the covers over your head and stay in bed forever. The wind was tearing around Tommy's corner of the house making a low whistling sound as the wind caught the drainpipes, and the trees. Tommy couldn't see whether it was snowing or not. There was frost on the window - the inside of the window! It must be snowing; well, he hoped that it was snowing - snowing so hard that school would be canceled. P L E A S E let my school be on the list of "school closings" which was being announced just then on the radio. Tommy snuggled lower in the bed when he heard the dreaded call from the kitchen:

"Tommy, it's 7 o'clock. Come on. Get out of bed. You'll be late!" It was his mother, of course, and yes, school was open.

"I'm coming" he called out loud. "Aww, rats!" he mumbled under the sheets - those nice warm sheets. Dressed only in his underpants, Tommy mustered all his courage, then threw back the bed covers and made the dash to the bathroom.

"Ahhh, it's freezing!" he yelled as he hurled himself down the hall to the bathroom hunched over and hugging himself along the way.

The tile floor in the bathroom felt like a sheet of ice. Tommy jumped up and down trying hard not to keep any foot on the floor for longer than a millisecond.

"It's fffrreeeezing!"

When he finally straightened up to look in the mirror, he was sure that he could see the reflection of his goose bumps they were so large. He looked down at his toes; yes, they were still there but they looked a pale blue.

"I hate winter!" he yelled into the face in the mirror. "I'm not pitching for any team where it's cold," he decided now and forever.

"Make sure you wash behind your ears, and your neck, and don't forget your face," his mother called out even as Tommy was looking in the mirror mouthing the same words and wagging his head from side to side mimicking her: "...wash behind your ears, and your neck, and don't forget your face."

She said that every morning; even on Saturdays when you weren't supposed to wash. Tommy ran the water hard enough so that his mother could hear it, but there was no way that Tommy was going to wash today. The thought of hot water running down the back of his neck and turning colder as it made its way down the small of his back made him shiver. His skin was about to explode in a shower of a billion goose bumps all over the bathroom floor. Nope, there would be no washing today. He dashed back to the bedroom.

He was about to jump into yesterday's comfy, but only slightly soiled shirt, trousers and socks, when his mother called out her second pre-breakfast directive: "And make sure, you put on a clean shirt and trousers. And for heaven's sake, P L E A S E change those socks!"

"Yes, mother," he intoned, even as he rolled his eyes. "How did she know that?" he thought to himself. "A hidden camera, maybe. That's got to be it."

"Well, don't you look dashing today," she said proudly as Tommy shuffled and stumbled into the kitchen.

Tommy was a handsome young boy with soft and gentle features although slightly built, with a somewhat fragile appearance. His sandy hair tumbled down his forehead and almost into his eyes. Yes, it was his eyes, she thought, that was his most endearing characteristic. They were round, dark brown and surrounded by long dark lashes. But in a way, they were also sad eyes. Certainly, not from any sad experience that she could remember. And yet, you couldn't help look twice and see a sadness there; a sadness perhaps from things to come. She shook off the feeling and came over to him; gave him a hug, and then bent to kiss him on the top of his head. She held him close to her for a moment. No special reason, just one of the mysterious and wondrous feelings that only mothers have but can never describe in words.

"You know, Tommy, I love you," she said as she felt a tear welling in her eyes and taking a deep swallow.

"I love you, too, mom." Then, he looked up at her. "But could you tell me how you knew I was going to put on yesterday's shirt and socks?"

She tossed her head back and laughed. "Aha, it's a secret that only mothers know," she said as she gently nudged him toward the table.

After the daily duel with his mother over whether breakfast should consist of Chocomonsters and Bubbleberry Tarts washed down with a glass of Spaceman's Orange drink, a duel he generally lost, he settled for grain cereal and a muffin.

"Tastes like lawnmower mush," he muttered just low enough so that his mother couldn't quite catch it. But she did send him a motherly protective scowl.

He managed the muffin and the cereal, but when she turned to sip her coffee, he gulped down the murky orange liquid fortified with a horrific number of chemical additives. She knew he would, of course, but she stayed with her back turned long enough to allow him to drink the horrible mixture without choking on it.

"OK, kiddo, it's time. Do you have your homework, your keys, your lunch money?" This was the last of the daily pre-school rituals Tommy had to endure. "Yes, mom."

"Remember, that I'm going to be a bit late getting home from work today. Will you be all right by yourself?"

"I'll be OK, mom."

"And, one more thing...

"Yes, mom, I know," he said wearily, "Homework first, and no Killer Gorilla cartoons."

"Tommy!"

"OK, OK. I promise."

"There's the bus. Quick, Tommy. Give me a kiss. Have fun today."

"'Bye, mom. See ya later," he said cheerily as he ran out the door. Just as suddenly, he stopped in his tracks, "OOPS!" He turned and ran back to see his mother standing in the door with his book bag in her outstretched arms, shaking her head. With a sheepish grin, he grabbed the bag and started toward the bus which was waiting with door open and an impatient driver scowling at him.

He gingerly inched his way along the frozen foot path balancing himself with his arms outstretched like a tight rope walker, but instead of a balance beam, he carried a yellow Chocomonster lunch pail. At the foot of the bus step, he turned quickly, waved at his mother, and yelled out above the howling wind, "Bye, Mom!"

Later, she told her own mother that she would see his face forever as he turned before getting on the bus. She would never forget it. His smile framed in the snowy mist with chunky flakes covering his jacket and turning his hair white. ("Aw, Mom, it's not cool to walk on the bus with your hood up.") For an instant, his eyes sparkled like the snow and the sadness disappeared. For as many times as he said his good-byes in the morning, he never failed to turn at the foot of the bus steps to look at her and wave one final "Bye, Mom!" That was her favorite and the most special good-bye; and the one she would remember until her dying day.

CHAPTER 2

Tommy's house was the last stop on the driver's route on the way to the Pine Creek School which was about thirty miles away. It was a forty-five minute drive on the best of days. Between Tommy's house and the school was the open prairie that stretched as far as the eye could see, broken only by a pencil straight road that disappeared into the horizon. The stark beauty of the Midwest Plains was redolent with the perfume of prairie flowers in summer, but transformed into a barren and harsh tundra in the winter.

Today, the driver knew that the storm which was worsening by the minute would require at least double the driving time and treble the patience. She was carrying a load of young kids taunting each other; hurling books and even toast with jam; and teasing with tit for tat jibes. Then there were demands that she arbitrate each petty dispute through the rear view mirror, while keeping both eyes on the road and both hands on the wheel. This morning's ride was going to be a challenge indeed. Her nerves were already frayed as she negotiated the bad roads to Tommy's house which couldn't be plowed fast enough in the face of the heavy snow swirling around in ever growing mountainous drifts.

Margie Baker had been driving school buses for fifteen years, but today, she wasn't happy. Something inside her told her that this day would not end well. "Why," she thought, "Why was it necessary to be in school today? What harm would come to their education if they spent the day off, romping in the snow? Pushing these kids; that's what they were doing. Baby overachievers who would turn out to be adult neurotics, dulling their senses with a mix of vodka and happy pills."

Margie was short in stature; a robust woman with faded carrot red hair done in tight curls together with liberal streaks of grey at her temples. Her ruddy complexion spoke of years working as a riveter in the shipyard sun; and her round face was sprinkled with a mix of freckles and the dark brown spots common to someone of her years. She had particularly large forearms forged as a riveter in her younger days. With keen, blue eyes, she wore a serious, no-nonsense expression most of the time. She was a woman of few words. But, for as resolute and determined as she appeared, she had a warm and special feeling for her passengers - "my little tikes", she confided to one of her very few close friends. And in her fifteen years, she had driven most of the young people in the county at one time or another.

She had the gift of infinite patience, particularly at 8 o'clock on a rainy Monday morning in a chilly and damp yellow school bus - or at least that's what they thought. She chuckled to herself. It really wasn't patience after all; she had loads of that. No, it was all those years in the Navy shipyard in Newport News, Virginia where she had lost part of her hearing owing to the constant clamor of hammers against steel hulls.

She had been one of the few women riveters in the business. She never thought of herself as a pioneer for women. She was just a good riveter with a great job, good pay and lots of fresh air. She had even met her husband in that melee of welders, riveters, and crane operators. She'd had a good life with him and their son, until Vietnam. Even to this day, she could sometimes hear the clanging of the hammers, and it never failed to bring a small smile to her face. The partial hearing loss was what led to her early retirement; and it was that same partial hearing loss which helped her keep her wits about her when the noise level in the bus would reach a crescendo. Well, she was retired now and it didn't matter to her what they thought. She was comfortable now with herself as grandmother figure to the kids. She rather liked the sobriquet the kids had bestowed on her: "Grandma Margie". This would be the closest she could come to actually being a grandmother ever since her son Gavin had died in Vietnam. She drew up her shoulders to take in a deep breath and then let it and the sadness of Gavin out. Anyway, she thought, the pay here was good too, the hours reasonable and, more importantly, everyone knew her and trusted their kids to her driving skill.

Today more than any other would tax "Grandma Margie" behind the wheel of the old yellow machine.

"Good morning, Grandma Margie," Tommy said barely above the din the bus.

Grandma Margie read his lips. "Hello, Tommy. Find a seat, and stay put, OK, Tommy. This is going to be a long ride today." The last sentence she muttered more to herself than to Tommy who had quickly found his usual seat two rows behind Grandma Margie and along side his best friend, Mark Lowell.

"Hi, Mark, did you see the 'Super Jets' show last night?"

Mark was sullen and after several moments could only grumble, "No, I got in trouble and had to go to my room."

Tommy could hardly contain his enthusiasm. He was disappointed that Mark hadn't seen the movie, but wanted to share it with his friend. "Gee, that's too bad, it was really great. They had this really neat plane that no one can see on radar; you know like the Klingon's cloaking shield."

"Shut up, Tommy, will ya", Mark shot back. Just as Tommy was about to be stung by his friend's remark, Tracey Morley leaned over from her seat ahead and said, "Yea, and did you see the way the plane takes off. Do they let girls fly in those planes?"

Tommy screwed up his nose and was puzzled for a moment. "Yea, I guess so. Why not?" Mark was not about to let anyone interfere with his sulk: "No, they don't, Tracey. Girls don't know anything about jet bombers." The rejoinder was immediate: "Oh, yes, they do. They know just as much as boys." And so it went, their voices mixing in this rolling pandemonium.

Grandma Margie didn't hear much of the racket; and she never once looked in the rear view mirror to see whose breakfast was winging its way across the bus. Her face was chiseled with concentration. Her arms ached as she fought with the bus as it began to fall victim to the ice and snow. Once easy roads, mostly straight and direct, were now disappearing in the thickening snow. Where the road ended and the shoulder began became an experienced guess - and one requiring increasingly more prayer. She knew she should carry a small portable radio just for days like this, but it would probably be useless anyway. Who could possibly hear anything in this four-wheel Tower of Babel!

CHAPTER 3

At the same time she saw Tommy's bus disappear in the swirl of blinding snow, Joanna Flagg heard the radio announce a change in school closings. Pine Creek School was now closed in the face of what was certainly a major winter storm. Another blunder by the weatherman, she thought. All the buses that had already arrived, would, after a brief respite for the drivers, turn around for the return trip. A shiver of fear went through Joanna as she heard the urgency in the radio announcer's voice: "Parents should advise bus drivers who may not have heard this message not to attempt to make the journey to Pine Creek School. The roads are becoming impassable, blinding snow and drifting conditions are in effect. Parents in the outlying communities of High Ridge, Carter's Creek and Ellenville are warned to stay indoors."

Just then, Scott Flagg, Tommy's father, came in looking like the Abominable Snowman. His normally dark beard and mustache were now frozen snowy white; and his eyebrows also looked like they had been sprayed white for the occasion. A tall man, he framed the door. He began pounding his feet on the thick mat and slapping himself to allow the snow to fall off his jacket and trousers.

"Jo, it's impossible to move out there; the snow is dropping faster by the minute. I think we've already lost a few head of cattle that wandered off from the pen in the middle of the night. By the way, where's Tommy? He must be happy that he got a day off." When he saw the look on his wife's face, he knew in an instant and shared her mounting fear. "They let the bus go...in this?" He sounded incredulous. She nodded ruefully. "I'll go look for the bus," he added quickly.

"No, Scott, please don't. I don't want both of you out there. I'm already sick with worry. If anything happens, none of those kids could stand the cold for very long."

"Now, Jo, don't go making it worse than it is. I'm sure they're OK. Grandma Margie is the best. She'll take it very slow. She'll get there, and then give them all hell for not canceling school earlier. Worse comes to worse, the kids will probably spend the night in the gym. They'll have a great time; no parents; no curfew; lots of junk food; and best of all, we get free baby-sitting service."

He gave her a mischievous look, "We'll have the night alone - just the two of us, snuggled up by a fire. What do you think?"

He put his arm around her shoulder, but he knew that she was already too frightened to see the romance; and after looking out the window again, he wasn't too sure himself.

CHAPTER 4

White-out.

Margie stopped the bus; put on her anorak, pulled up her hood and went out the door. She stood in front of the bus and was amazed that she had come this far. She admitted to herself that she had done it by memory alone. She had come down these roads so many times before, that she had driven only with a mental image of the road. No, she wasn't lost; but she couldn't see beyond the hood of the yellow bus which itself was now piled under snow despite the heat from the engine. For the first time in all her years of driving, she was frightened. She knew that she couldn't keep this up much longer; her mental map was good but she could not trust it for the next twenty-five miles. That meant she had only gone five miles in an hour! She was already exhausted physically and mentally. She could not turn around. The roads here were too narrow for that. Her best course was to press ahead; stopping to rest every now and then.

"Just take it slow, Margie baby. You can do this," she kept saying to herself. But even as she did so, she knew that she was running on her reserves. If she could only put her head down for a moment; close her eyes and have a little rest.

The children, for as young as they were, could sense the increasing danger in their situation and the strain on Grandma Margie. For some time, the conversations had become muted; the teasing and taunting ceased. Most just sat there, staring out, into what could only have reminded them of looking into a glass of milk. But this wasn't milk, and there were no cookies. No mommies and daddies and cozy kitchens - just the bus; the cold which kept creeping in despite the heater; and the snow, ...and more snow. Slowly, each child in turn began to feel in the pit of his or her stomach a sense of primal fear; the fear of the unknown; and for some in private, the fear of death.

argie reboarded the bus, Shelly Mesner, her lower lip quivering, asked in a hesitant and frail voice, "Grandma Margie, is everything all right. Are we going to make it OK?"

One of the older boys in the rear seized the opportunity to frighten little Shelly even further, and in some perverse way confront his own fear:

"No, Shelly welly, we're all going to freeze to death. F R R E E E Z E." He drew the last word out slowly and ominously with his hand cupped around his mouth to create a deep base tone which filled the quiet bus. And for an instant, everyone, even Margie, felt the word, F R R E E E Z E.

Margie put the bus in low gear and started to inch forward. As she released the clutch of the old standard transmission vehicle, the pain in her left leg was becoming acute. The windshield wipers were fighting a losing battle against snow driven in a furry against her window.

Just then, she felt the bus rise up to meet the incline in the road. She pictured it in her mind. She could see this very stretch of the road in the Spring with all the wild daisies along side the road. The road went higher, the incline a little steeper.

"Yes, yes," she said aloud. "That's it; right; we're OK. I know where we are. Yup, I remember that spot."

The bus was climbing. It was holding the road. Yes, we're going to make it. Yes, we are definitely going to make it. She almost didn't notice that the windshield wipers had all but given up. There was just a little hole. But she wasn't looking anyway. She could, no, had to, see it in her mind map.

The bus crested the hill. Margie breathed a sigh of relief. She rewarded herself with a two minute break. Each few yards was a victory; a conquest over the fury that raged outside. The back of her neck and her shoulders ached so that she hunched her shoulders up against her neck, closed her eyes and slowly, almost painfully, turned her head from side to side. She took a deep breath, flexed her fingers and re-gripped the steering wheel. Slowly, ever so slowly, she let out the clutch pedal. Suddenly, the bus lurched forward. Maybe, it was that after so much use that day and for years before, the gears had given out; maybe it was that her leg gave out. She didn't know; and just then it really didn't matter. She slammed on the brake, telling herself, " No, Margie; easy, Margie baby, easy on the brake; nice and easy." She could feel the sweat in her cap; her throat went parched dry.

But it was too late. And she knew it.

The bus lurched over the crest of the hill. The brakes locked the wheels. For the longest instant, the bus looked straight down the other side of the hill, as if it were frozen in time. It reminded Margie of being on the roller coaster at the summer fair. At the moment when the front half of the roller coaster is poised at the first long drop waiting for the back end to catch up. And then it began to inch forward; then two; then a foot. A little more and then it started to gather momentum. Margie straightened the wheels and kept pumping the brakes, but nothing happened. The bus started down the hill on a sharp angle. Margie was furiously working the wheel. She hoisted up as hard as she could on the emergency brake, but that only had the effect of forcing the bus to turn completely sideways to the road. Faster and faster, it slipped sideways. Margie wasn't driving the bus any longer. It seemed to be driving itself...more momentum, and ever closer to the end.

Margie cursed. In those last few moments, it almost felt as if some evil white demon began pushing the bus faster and faster down the hill. "This can't be happening; this can't be happening," she raged at the now snow covered windshield.

Margie gunned the engine and straightened the wheels in one last desperate attempt to take control of this beast. But it was not to be. The spinning rear wheels shrieked but could not find any traction. And it only succeeded in turning the bus once again - this time facing backwards down the hill. Now the front of the bus began to whipsaw violently back and forth. Margie turned back to look at the children. She could see them holding on to their seats, and to each other. Their mouths were formed in screams but she could not hear them. Time began to slow down in these last moments. She could actually see Shelly Mesner's eyes blinking slower now. She saw Tommy and suddenly thought about her own son, Gavin, who had died in Vietnam. "He was so young, like Tommy, in fact he looks like Tommy."

At that instant, the rear wheels of the bus hit the side of the road, jerking the front of the bus violently around facing down the hill again. But it did not stop. With that last violent twist, the momentum carried the bus off the side of the road and then flipped on its side into a headlong plunge down the ravine.

Before the darkness came, Margie was thrown from her seat and slammed against the door. In the last few seconds before she lost consciousness, she whispered, "Hello, Gavin, you look so much like Tommy...," and then nothing.

The bus slid down into the ravine like a sled in a giant luge. The yellow of the bus mingled with the spray of ice and snow billowing in its path. Evergreen trees snapped in the wake of the yellow giant that had now turned on its back. With its black wheels up, it plummeted deeper in the ravine like a dying whale. The screech of twisting metal and shattering glass mixed with the thunder of several tons of bus falling down and down into the ravine, and sent echoes screaming off the rock walls.

It drowned out the cries, and screams of the young cargo being thrown about like rag dolls cast aside by a petulant child. Limbs flailed, trying in desperation to grab for something, anything. But there was nothing...just yellow empty space turning and churning and filling with snow. Their screams mingled with the scream of metal and the shattering of glass. Wide terrified eyes formed their own silent screams because terror choked off any sound.

At the bottom of the ravine, the bus stopped its hellish ride. The thundering stopped as quickly as it had started. Now – silence; like the silence just before dawn. No sounds at all. No birds; no wind in the trees. Not even the whisper of a breath. Nothing.

Then, like the morning after a very dark night, daylight and time began to catch up to the young hapless victims who had endured a lifetime of terror in about thirty seconds. They were in real time now, and that realization burst on them like a fireworks explosion on the 4th of July...and painfully.

CHAPTER 5

The sheriff of Pine Creek had personally taken the calls of parents who were by now terrified to the limit awaiting the arrival of their children at the school. "Yes, the Carter's Creek school bus had arrived; and the High Ridge bus is just getting in now. No, Mrs. Flagg, Ellenville hasn't arrived yet, but we're sure they'll get here. After all, Margie's at the wheel. We'll call you as soon as it arrives."

Joanna Flagg turned to her husband, "Scott, there's something wrong. I just know it. It's been three hours since they left here. The High Ridge bus has the same distance to go over the same kind of roads. Scott, I know it. I'm so frightened. Scott, what can we do?"

"Look, Joanna, let's wait another few minutes. We'll try the sheriff again. If they're not at the school by then, we'll take the snowmobiles and follow Margie's route. We all know it. OK?"

She nodded, and smiled thinly. Joanna looked at the clock on the mantle and made a mental note to count the "few minutes". All she could hear was the ticking of the clock that seemed to fill the room. She paced the living room and glanced over at the clock after every few strides. Yes, she was certain now that something was wrong. She could feel it.

"Tommy, oh, my Tommy, what has happened?", she whispered softly.

"Hello, this is Sheriff Kanter. Oh, hello, Mr. Flagg. No, I'm sorry, we haven't heard from them. Yes, I'm worried too. They should have been here by now. Yes, OK. I agree with you. You start on your end; and we'll do the same here. And let's pray that we find them in between." Scott Flagg immediately called the other parents who were by this time ready to mount the search using snowmobiles, a common vehicle for Midwest farmers. They agreed to meet at Scott Flagg's house.

Within moments, a caravan of 10 parents seated aboard growling snowmobiles had formed up outside the Flagg's house. All the faces were tense with the anticipation of the search. Not a word was spoken as Scott mounted his snowmobile. With a silent signal from Scott, they launched themselves into the blinding snow and quickly disappeared in the whiteness. Joanna Flagg sat huddled behind Scott to protect herself from the driving snow which felt like needles against her skin already bruised from the cold.

ugh she was not more than inches from his head, she had to shout her question above the roar of the wind and the whine of snowmobile engines. She asked it more to assure herself than for any specific answer: "Scott, what do you think? Where are they?"

Scott leaned his head back and over his left shoulder shouted, "My guess is that they never made the hill at

White Bluff...probably couldn't get the traction to get up the hill."

He couldn't tell her, but there was another possibility too terrifying to contemplate: they made the hill but didn't make it down the other side, where a narrow road and bridge crossed the ravine. He didn't have to say anything. Joanna Flagg could fill in the blanks herself.

One of the snowmobiles careened off the road, tipped over throwing both driver and rider. No one was injured but that little incident sent knowing glances to everyone. Something had gone very wrong with the bus. Now, they all knew it. And what's more, they could feel it.

"All right, let's mount up. Everybody ready?"

The group moved ahead, slower this time, but no less determined. Scott was the lead. So long as he could see the lonely tire tracks, now almost filled in with snow, he knew that everything was all right. He wiped the snow from his goggles and for a moment imagined what is was like for Grandma Margie behind the wheel of the bus. His thoughts came quickly back to the search as he felt the engine strain to meet the incline of the hill. Soon now...it would be soon; and it would be bad.

CHAPTER 6

They crested the hill on their snowmobiles in time to see the fireball shoot up into the sky, followed seconds later by a thunderous roar that they both heard and felt. "Oh, my God, oh my God. Tommy. The children," Joanna Flagg screamed.

For a second, all they could do was stare, mouths wide open, frozen in horror. The vibrations from the explosion shook them to their senses. The group of parents jumped from their snowmobiles and frantically began running, stumbling, or falling down the ravine in the path left by the bus in a desperate rush to reach the children. From their vantage point, they could see the children strewn about. Dressed in different colored jackets, they resembled little dolls under a green Christmas tree decorated in white.

In the middle of this tableau was the burning school bus.

The children looked up to hear the shouts of their parents as they saw them plowing down the steep ravine. The closer they came, the more the children began to allow themselves to vent their fear and pain. Several began to cry and scream. The parents were themselves in a frenzy of fear and frustration as the deep snow thwarted their urgency in trying to reach their children.

Mothers and fathers began to call out names. "Jonathan, where are you?" "Larry...Larry!" "Mary...Judith!"

Amy and Frank Lowell saw Jason kneeling in the deep snow cradling Mark in his arms and crying. Mark was not moving. "Mom, Dad, I tried...I really tried...I'm sorry." Frank scooped up Mark, saw the blue face; and immediately lowered the child to the ground, opened his mouth. He put his own mouth over Mark's and with his large, powerful right hand began to push rhythmically on the little boy's chest in synch with puffs of his breath. Amy took her coat off and wrapped it around Jason whose body was shaking uncontrollably from both the cold, the pain and sobbing for his little brother. They both watched as Frank Lowell ministered to Mark. Puff, push...puff, push. "Breathe, Mark. Breathe, boy."

Children were quickly reunited with parents who were removing coats and hats to put on their children. They had to do something, anything.

Joanna Flagg's head and body jerked from side to side as she called out, "Tommy, Tommy...my baby. Where are you? Tommy! Oh, God...Tommy." Her eyes were bulging and she kept running from one reunited family to another. "Larry, Larry...did you see Tommy?" Larry could only shake his head no. Then to Marty, and Catlin..."Did you see him?" The reply was the same and for an instant she thought she would go crazy, "No, Mrs. Flagg, I didn't see him." Then, she remembered. Mark. Mark Lowell. He always sits with Mark. She started to call for Mark, then saw Frank Lowell leaning over the unconscious

Mark. She was beside herself. She cupped her hands over her mouth. She was trying desperately not to scream.

Jason Lowell saw the look of terror and desperation. "Mrs. Flagg. They were sitting together, up front. I dug Mark out from the window over there," Jason called out pointing to middle of the bus.

She wheeled around and saw that her husband was running toward the bus. He had to get there before his wife. Several of the other parents looked up and realized that there was only one child unaccounted for: Tommy.

The rear of the bus was still partly packed with melting snow. The front part was charred; most of the windows had shattered; several seats were still smoldering. Scott dropped to his knees and poked his head in at the front end of the bus. Nothing. He ran to the rear and tried to open the rear emergency door. It wouldn't open. He pulled and pulled. It wouldn't budge. He raged at the door; he began kicking at it with his massive boots. It loosened the packed snow and with a last effort summoned up from fear and frustration, the door opened. He tore at the seats that were in his path; and pawed at the snow, trying to feel for the signs of his son. Nothing. He was driven. Joanna got in behind him and started to look more thoroughly. Catlin Toomey's mother climbed in, then another parent. Several positioned themselves at the entrance, hushed now and waiting. But the worst was yet to come.

Scott almost missed it. From the corner of his eyes now wet with tears, he saw the yellow spot. Yellow. What was it he saw in the kitchen that was yellow....that's it! The Chocomonster lunch box! Scott dove at the spot and with bare hands began scooping the snow. He found the lunch box at the same time that he saw a small hand, Tommy's hand, still gripping the lunch box. For moment, he was amazed, "He loved that stupid Chocomonster's lunch box so much, he actually hung on to it through all this."

He shook his head and then called out, "I found him. I got him. Joanna!"

Joanna Flagg stumbled behind Scott and dug out Tommy's legs and his left arm which was at his side. The top half of Tommy was lying under one of the seats. It's what saved his life. For some unexplained reason, the seat and probably the seat in front had acted as a barrier preventing snow from piling in on Tommy who was tossed under the seat.

But they were not prepared for what they saw.

Tommy was lying face down. Scott could see his little chest moving up and down. Thank God! He's alive. "He's alive...he's alive," he shouted to Joanna; to everyone.

Scott turned Tommy over. "He's ...," but in an instant his elation turned to horror. "Oh my God, no...no."

His father stared for a moment; then began shaking his head violently from side to side and dropped his head on Tommy's chest, "Oh, no...oh, no...Tommy....Tommy."

Joanna leaned over his shoulder, and then screamed. It was a scream from a nightmare. Her eyes rolled up and in a flash of white, she fell to her knees.

Tommy's face was burned beyond recognition.

In the distance, they heard the sheriff's siren. It too seemed to scream out the horror.

CHAPTER 7

It seemed like an eternity before the sheriff arrived. He found an area that resembled killing field. The snow had started to abate and that permitted the helicopter called in by the sheriff to land with a "triage team"; a team of doctors and nurses trained in administering emergency care in the field. A battle had indeed been fought here - a battle between life and death. Life was the overall winner; Grandma Margie was not so lucky. All but the worst injured were brought back up to the road to await the ambulances. The triage team led by Doctor Marion Blanchard, descended into the ravine to treat the three who could not be moved. Mark Lowell had revived momentarily but had passed out again. Mary Lyon was in agony and bleeding badly from her open leg break. Tommy was in the worst condition.

The triage team quickly inserted an airway into Mark, a tube slipped easily down his throat allowing him to breath. After being attached to a portable respirator his breaths came easily and the color in his cheeks became pinkish. An IV, an intravenous tube, was also inserted in his vein. The team moved quickly and quietly on to Mary. She was given several injections and an intravenous inserted to replace the enormous amount of blood loss. Her leg was put in what resembled a large air bag.

When they came to Tommy they found the little boy's blistered face and neck were charred black with pink and red blotches. What was left of his hair was in small clumps. His eyebrows and eyelashes were gone. His features were bloated; his lips were swollen and bruised. His left ear was torn. His breathing came fitfully. At times he gasped, and his breathing sounded raspy. His body shivered with each breath; and each breath was agonizingly painful. He was slipping away.

"Quick, let's get an airway started. He's in bad shape." The triage leader's voice was urgent. "OK, good. John, give me his vitals - pulse, BP, and temperature; Lou, I need an IV. Start with Ringer's lactate"

"Tommy, Tommy," Doctor Blanchard whispered in his ear, "Stay with me, Tommy, stay with us."

Joanna stood behind the team, her left hand over her mouth desperately trying not to cry out. Tears streamed down her cheeks. Scott had his arm around her trying to help her control her shaking. They could only watch helplessly. They could see the team working quickly and wordlessly on Tommy. Joanna could feel Tommy's pain as he reacted to the tube and the needles. "Oh, Tommy, oh my Tommy," she whispered. She buried her face into Scott's jacket and sobbed uncontrollably, her shoulders heaving as she did so. Scott stared straight ahead with an expression that looked like a granite mask as he fought back an urge to cry, but he had to remain strong for his wife...and for Tommy.

Doctor Blanchard leaned over Tommy searching for any other injuries. She found none. She looked up at Scott and Joanna with a mixture of sadness, concern and determination in her eyes. She was not going to lose him.

Tommy's airway was hooked into a respirator. He stopped gasping...and for a moment, Joanna thought .... Doctor Blanchard said without looking up at Tommy's parents, but sensing their concern, "Don't worry, we're breathing for him." She turned quickly to one of the nurses, "He's in pain. A good sign. Let's give him something for it. There are no other apparent injuries. Let's get him wrapped up in these blankets." She turned to look into the growing crowd of parents, sheriff deputies and medical personnel at the scene, looking for the communications coordinator. "Bill, Bill Jenkins, where are you. I need you here, now!"

"Yes, doctor," Bill called out as he ran over to her.

"Bill, call County General Hospital; tell them to have the burn unit ready. Tell them we have a child, male, about 10 years of age, with third degree burns on his face and neck. No other injuries visible, but strong possibility of respiratory complications. Tell them we've got an airway. He's on Ringer's lactate and morphine. Ask for any advice. Priority One, Bill."

Bill understood and began the call. "Oh, and Bill, tell the chopper pilot to stand-by for an air evac of these three kids."

Doctor Blanchard motioned to several deputies who gingerly lifted Tommy into a basket, and began the slow trek back up the ravine to the waiting helicopter. Doctor Blanchard turned, went over to Joanna and Scott and put her arms around both, "Hang in there. He's going to make it. He's burned pretty badly, but all in all, I'd say we're lucky...very lucky." Joanna and Scott started up the hill together with the other parents behind the three rescue baskets.

At the top of the hill, the three remaining parents could see ambulances, doctors and nurses scurrying from child to child; sheriff deputies, rescue personnel; and flashing blue, red and yellow lights. The helicopter was being loaded with its torn and tattered, but precious cargo. Joanna turned around and looked down the ravine and could see the overturned bus. This was no dream. It was a nightmare turned real. And as the helicopter lifted off, the nightmare had only just begun.

CHAPTER 8

He suddenly realized he was hearing sounds. Soft whirring sounds; beeping sounds; and faraway voices. Weird, he thought. The last sounds he heard were those in the bus, but somehow, he couldn't quite put his finger on it. It seemed so long ago. It was like a dream. Where was it...? he wondered.

He then began to smell things. That was strange too, because the last thing he remembered smelling was gasoline. Now, it smelled weird. He thought he was wrinkling his nose. What was that odor...where had he smelled that stuff before? Yes, it was coming back...it was...it was like his mom's floor cleaner. His mom. Yes, mom. He had a mom. He started to remember his mom, breakfast, the snow, ... it was coming back slowly now...his room, the cold....

"Make sure you wash behind your ears, and your neck, and don't forget your face;"

"...and for heaven's sake, P L E A S E change those socks!"

"You know, Tommy, I love you."

Faster and faster, the pictures, sounds and smells started to come back. Then, they came in a torrent of explosive flashes. His mother's face burst into his mind. The bus! The bus, the screams; kids' faces flying around inside the bus; the bus falling; snow in his face; the crush of the seats on top of him. He had tried to get up but the seats were on top of him. He called for help but no one heard him. Then, the smell of gasoline, and then...a whoosh...a flash of light and the burning in his face and in his throat and then...nothing.

Now he was here. But where was here? *Where am I?*

And then it struck him. It was like the same bright burning light that he felt before it got dark. Mostly, he remembered the pain. The bus, Grandma Margie, Shelly screaming...Oh, the pain. He could feel himself falling. He smelled the gasoline; then the bright light. His face was burning; his throat hurt so much. He was falling again. He had to stop himself. He tried to grab out to the seat, to reach out to hold on. The bus was falling. Mark was falling.

"Tommy...Tommy."

I have to stop falling. Can't see Grandma Margie, Mark, Catlin. Where are they? Can't see anything.

Tommy...Tommy. It's Mom."

Mark, Mark, where are you...Mom? Mom, is that you?

His arms flailed out in a vain attempt to hold on, but something was stopping him. Something was attached to his hands. *Where am I? Where is everybody? I can't see anybody. Am I dead? Anybody! Anybody! Mommy, mommy, where are you?*

"Tommy, Tommy. It's all right. Tommy. It's Mommy. I'm here. I'm right here. Do you feel me? I have your hand. It's OK. It's OK." She spoke softly, soothingly into his ear.

His arms and legs were thrashing but his limbs were in restraints in order to ensure that tubes and catheters, and his bandages would stay in place. He screamed...rather, he tried to scream, but nothing happened. He couldn't make sounds. His mother heard a series of grunts. She looked at the nurse and then to Scott who was seated at the foot of the bed.

Tommy screamed louder; but nothing came out. His mother heard the grunts become more agitated. The little boy's chest heaved. His whole body was jerking violently. It seemed as if he would break the restraints at any moment.

He fought to hold on as the bus screeched its way again down the ravine forcing Tommy to relive those last horrifying moments. Yet, he knew that somehow his mother was now there with him, but she wasn't on the bus that morning. She was supposed to be home. Now she was here with him. *But where is here. Where am I?*

Mommy, mommy. Please, mommy, help me. Where are you?

He turned his head from side to side to look for his mother. But he couldn't see her. But she was here. He could hear her. *Where are you? Why can't I see you?*

"Tommy, you're safe now. You're in the hospital. You had an accident. Tommy? It's OK. It's Mommy. And

Daddy is here too. You're safe. We have you. Don't be afraid."

His mother took his hand in hers. It looked so small and helpless. It was black and blue from the IV needles. Scott came around to take his other hand.

"Tommy, it's Daddy, Tommy. It's OK, it's OK. We're here with you.   There's no more bus.   It's all over. Everyone is OK."

Joanna Flagg wanted to touch her son so that he could feel her and know that it was going to be all right. But there was no place to touch. Tommy's face and neck were entirely covered with bandages leaving only enough space for the ventilator tube to exit his mouth. Another tube disappeared in the bandages around his nose. His eyes were covered in large puffy bandages. All she could think of was that her poor Tommy was a mass of wires, needles and probes all connected to monitors that kept silent watch with her.

It had been three long days, sitting and waiting. She watched as the ventilator had taken over Tommy's breathing. She watched the monitors day and night. She watched the clear liquid in the bag hanging above Tommy's head, sending a steady drip, drip into the I.V. that went in the back of Tommy's left hand.

Tommy had heard his mother and father. And at the same time he began to feel the effects of the next dose of pain medication. *Mommy, Daddy...Mommy, Daddy...Mom..m..y ....D.a..d..d...y.* He slept for another three days.

His mother put her head down on her chest. "I think I'll take a little nap...for a few minutes." As she fell asleep, for the first time she let her hand slip from Tommy's..."...just a few minutes." She too slept for the remainder of the day. Scott Flagg sat as if turned to stone. He would watch over the both of them. He would not let either of them out of his sight...not for a moment...not ever again.

CHAPTER 9

"Mom...,mom, are you there?"

"Yes, Tommy, I'm right here. I've got your hand."

"Mom, I can't see anything and my throat hurts." he said rasping. "When I swallow, it hurts. It feels like there's something in my throat."

"Yes, Tommy, that's because there was a tube in your throat to help you breathe."

"Mom, what happened?" He had to push each word out. "I don't remember...well, I sorta do. It was the bus. We went down the ravine. I don't much remember. Oh, yea, I felt the fire in my face and in my throat."

Joanna let him speak even though she knew it must be causing him pain to do so; the pain in his throat and the pain of remembering. But the doctor's said that it was best for him to confront it - little bits at a time. He was going to have a long road ahead of him. He didn't need to hurry. The effort was tiring him. He stopped. Joanna waited. She was waiting for him to ask...

"Mom?"

"Yes, Tommy."

"My eyes...I can't see."

"They've been bandaged, Tommy." It was time. She took a deep breath. She had to get this right. There would be no second chances. She looked over at Scott. He knew that it was time too. Scott nodded his OK.

"Tommy. Tommy, honey. You've had a very serious accident. You were right. The bus flipped over and went down the ravine. There was a fire and you were burned. Burned very badly." No, no. She made a face and thought to herself that she hadn't done it right. But how do you go about telling a ten year old that his face, and neck have been so badly burned; that some of the kids are in the hospital with broken bones and burns; and that Grandma Margie died. Worst of all, what was she going to tell him about his eyesight. Well, the doctors didn't know either. She shook her head and heaved a sigh.

"Am I blind?"

Tears were welling in her eyes. She was struggling. Who could ease *her* pain at seeing her baby burned, and in pain...and maybe blind. "No, Tommy, you're not blind," she lied. But she didn't know, did she? What else could she say? She was hoping that he didn't ask about his face and neck.

"Mom, what about the other kids?"

"Well, Tommy, lots of them were hurt, some badly. Some are here in the hospital; right now, same as you. Mary Lyon has a broken leg; Shelly Meisner was burned. Mark got hurt too - in his head. But everyone going's to be OK, thank God." She decided not to say anything about Grandma Margie. There would be a better time for that.

"Mom...I'm thirsty and I'm hungry."

For the first time in days, Joanna allowed herself a small smile. He's hungry, she thought. That's a good sign. "Tommy, I'm afraid that right now, all you can have is a little ice water. We'll have to wait until the doctor says it's OK."

"But, Mom, I'm hungry."

"I know Tommy, I know. Be patient."

Tommy called for his father in a voice that sounded more like a harsh whisper. "Yes, Tommy. I'm right here."

"Dad, did we lose any stock?" Tommy wanted to be a farmer like his Dad, but only in the off-season. First, he had to pitch for the major leagues.

"I'm afraid so. We lost three head when they wandered off in the blizzard. It could have been worse."

"One of them wasn't Winona, was it?" referring to his favorite cow.

Scott chuckled, "No, Tommy. Winona is fine and I'm sure missing you."

Tommy fell silent. Joanna watched his chest rise and fall rhythmically. He had fallen asleep. She looked over at Scott. He got up from where he had been sitting and living for most of these past five days. He rose slowly and painfully; walked over to his wife and put both his arms around her shoulders as she sat in the chair. "It's going to be OK, Jo, it's going to be OK."

He helped her out of her chair. They walked just outside Tommy's room and left the door open a crack so that they could see him. Then she broke down and really cried, letting out a flood of her own pain after six of the longest days in her life. How was she going to endure the rest? How was she going to be strong for her Tommy, for her family, for herself?

The next morning, Tommy's doctor came in. "Good morning, Tommy. It's Doctor Joe. How are you feeling this morning?" The doctor was flipping through the metal covered chart handed to him by the duty nurse. He was nodding, "Hmm, hmm...," and was about to tell the nurse...

"I'm hungry," Tommy complained. He would promise anything right now for a giant bowl of Chocomonsters. Truth was, he'd even settle for the lawn mower mush his mom made him eat.

"Hungry, uh. Well, let's see what we can do about that. First, let me have a look at you and then we can get you something. OK?" Known to the kids as Doctor Joe, Doctor Joseph Jankowski, was a specialist in treatment of burn victims. Together with his assistant, Gail Franklin, they gently lifted several of the bandages to check on the progress and to ensure there wasn't an infection. The doctor frowned and shook his head but needed to keep Tommy talking.

"Lookin' good, ace, lookin' good," Doctor Joe said to Tommy trying to sound cheerful. For all the years he practiced as a doctor, it was still painful for him to see the ravages of burns on young children. "Who's going to win the series this year, Chicago White Sox or the Blue Jays?"

"The Sox," Tommy said without hesitation.

"Think so? Well, I'll bet the Jays whip your Sox in four straight," Doctor Joe challenged.

"Oh, yea. The Jays don't have a pitcher who can go seven innings and they don't have long ball hitters," Tommy shot back. He was oblivious to Doctor Jankowski's probing his wounds. The doctor's frown continued, but only Gail Franklin could see it.

"So you think you want to eat, uh. How's your throat? Sore maybe?"

Tommy hesitated, but he was too hungry to care, "Well, it's a little sore, but not that bad."

"OK, Tommy. Let's give it a shot. "Gail, let's get this next Rookie of the Year Pitcher, a man sized breakfast, shall we," Doctor Joe said exaggerating. Gail nodded and knew from experience that it would have to be anything but Chocomonsters. Actually, it was going to be oatmeal and ice cream.

"Doctor Joe?" Tommy called. "What about my eyes? I can't see anything? Mom says I'm not blind but I can't see anything."

Doctor Jankowski sat at the edge of the bed. Gail Franklin went for the breakfast. "Well, Tommy. No, I don't think your blind either, but your eyes got burned as well as your face and neck. And because your eyes are so sensitive, we're going to have to keep them covered a little longer."

"Well, with these bandages, I feel like I'm blind." Tommy pouted.

"Just hang in there, ace. Trust me on this one."

Gail returned, nodded to the doctor, signaling her readiness to begin the morning's routine. "Tommy, this is Gail. I've ordered your breakfast, but I've got to be honest with you. It's not going to be Chocomonsters. It's more like a...

"Lawn mower mush," Tommy interrupted.

"I'm afraid so, Tommy. But before we do breakfast, I need to change your bandages. OK?"

"OK," Tommy said wearily.

Gail Franklin gently removed the bandages as Doctor Jankowski watched. The pained expressions which passed between them told them it was bad...very bad. "Ace, I gotta go visit another patient. I'll catch you later, probably tomorrow. Gail will stay with you to finish fixing your bandages."

Tommy waited a moment and then said, "Bye, Doctor Joe." But the doctor had already left the room.

As Gail was finishing, Joanna and Scott walked in. "Good morning, Gail, how's our favorite patient?" She knew that she could not tell them how bad Tommy's burns really were. The deep scarring which was clearly evident on both his face and neck; the awful damage to his nose; and his eyes...well, it was too early to tell about his eyes.

"You should be very proud, Mrs. Flagg. Tommy 's a very brave young man. We're making progress. Slow but sure." Gail didn't know what else to say.

Joanna went over to Tommy take his hands which were now free of the intravenous lines and gently pressed them against her cheeks, so she didn't notice Gail's expression which gave away the nurse's personal misgivings about Tommy's condition. But Scott saw it. "Gail, would you mind showing me Tommy's chart at the nursing station? I have a few questions," Scott said matter of factly. Gail knew why and prepared herself.

"OK, Gail. How is he really? How bad is it?" Scott looked hard into Gail's eyes when they were in the corridor.

Gail took a deep breath: "Well, Mr. Flagg, it's really hard to say at this point. He's very badly burned. And he's going to need lots of plastic surgery. I think he's out of danger from any complications, but I think the best thing, really, is to speak to Doctor Jankowski."

Scott softened and let his shoulders slump. Almost apologetically, he said, "Thanks, Gail. I know you and Doctor Joe are doing the best you can."

Tommy needed to remain in the hospital for one operation. It was to be the first of many.

"Guess what, Mom, I'm going to have a *skinwrap*."

"A what...?" his mother replied, looking nervously over to Doctor Jankowski.

"No, Tommy, *skin graft*," the doctor corrected laughing.

"Right, that's what I said. Doctor Joe is going to take some skin off my butt and put it on my face," Tommy said turning his head toward where he had heard his mother's voice. The bandages on his eyes had not come off yet.

"No, Tommy, that's not what I said," the doctor corrected again. "I said we have to **get off our butts** and do a skin graft soon. And we're going to take the skin from inside your arm."

Joanna smiled, looked at her son and then at the doctor, "Doctor Joe, I think he's feeling better. I'll bet he's looking for Chocomonsters."

"And hamburgers," the doctor added rolling his eyes and shaking his head. "But, it's a good sign." Just then, a sly impish grin came over the Doctor Joe's face.

Uh, oh, Gail thought. When he gets that look, he's just like a kid. He's up to no good.

Doctor Joe then went over to Tommy and whispered softly in his ear, "Listen, ace. I'll tell you what. If you go on being such a great patient, I'll sneak some Chocomonsters into you after the skin graft. And don't say anything. Whaddya think?"

Tommy listened intently as everyone watched with puzzled expressions, all that is except Gail. She knew it. He's acting the kid himself. "Awright!" Tommy exclaimed and for the first time smiled broadly.

Still in his conspiratorial whisper, Doctor Joe added, "OK, kid, this is between you and me." No one asked what the secret was. Tommy was still smiling.

As Doctor Jankowski left the room, he turned to everyone, "We're going with the skin graft. I put it on the schedule for tomorrow." And then turning to Tommy, "See ya, ace."

Tommy waved, still smiling. Chocomonsters, at last!

The surgery went smoothly and without any complications. Tommy's youth was his greatest asset now. He was certainly going to need it in the forthcoming weeks.

"Tommy...Tommy," Gail Franklin called softly.

From somewhere in the silent misty haze, Tommy could hear her. Slowly, he became more aware: the hospital, the fire and the burning on his face, the crash, falling...falling. Tommy's arms reached out. His little body arched upwards. He had to hold on to something. The bus was falling. His friends. He could see their faces. He heard the screams. He screamed, "Noooo".

"Tommy. Tommy! Ace. It's Doctor Joe. Ace!"

Both the doctor and his assistant held Tommy, preventing him from tearing at the bandages. Slowly, Tommy's shaking subsided. He was in the hospital. Doctor Joe and Nurse Gail were there. It was all right. The bus was gone. The fire was gone. Tommy's body went limp.

"Tommy, it's me, Doctor Joe"

Through parched lips, Tommy weakly nodded his head, "Hi, Doctor Joe. Is it over?"

"Yes, Tommy. It's over and you did very well."

"Can I have my Chocomonsters now," Tommy managed to utter the words and fell asleep. Gail shook her head. So that's what Doctor Joe was up to. Tommy slept fitfully for the remainder of that day.

Doctor Jankowski came in the next day to find Joanna and Scott Flagg talking to Tommy whose face was wrapped up but was otherwise chattering away to his parents. "Hi, Ace, how goes it?" he said to Tommy and nodding a greeting to his parents at the same time.

"OK, Doctor Joe, I guess."

"What do you mean, Tommy, 'I guess,'" the doctor asked as he squinted his eyes.

"My eyes, Doctor Joe. I want to see something. I know I can see. I can see white. Please Doctor Joe, can't we take these stupid things off."

"Yes, Tommy, they're coming off today. When you were in the operating room we checked your eyes and they're OK."

Joanna Flagg clasped her hands to her mouth as she drew in a sudden breath. "Oh, Tommy, that's great news."

Doctor Joe had that impish grin again when he looked at Tommy, "Well, what do you want first: Bandages off, or ..." the doctor paused for the dramatic effect. "...the Chocomonsters?"

Tommy was thrilled. More good news! The bandages off **and** the Chocomonsters. "Bandages first; so I can see the Chocomonsters," he put in quickly.

"Kids are a lot smarter than we give them credit for," Doctor Jankowski said to no one in particular. And with that, he very gently removed the bandages. Tommy squinted at first and then slowly opened his eyes to the fullest and there they were! Mom! Dad! Ah, that's what Doctor Joe and Gail look like! This was great! Tommy's excitement made his eyes sparkle.

"I can see!" Tommy exclaimed as he reached both hands out to his parents. He saw his mother crying. "Mom?"

"It's OK, Tommy. I'm all right. I'm crying because I'm so happy," his mother said between her tears

And then he saw them. At the foot of the bed, he could see Doctor Joe. He knew it had to be Doctor Joe because he was the one holding up a box, a large box, of Chocomonsters.

It was going to be a good day, Tommy thought. A very good day.

CHAPTER 10

After three weeks in the hospital and one skin graft later, the best thing now was to get Tommy back home, and then to school with his friends. It was also time for Tommy to face the entire truth about his accident and the extent of his injuries.

On his morning rounds, Doctor Jankowski and Gail Franklin met Joanna and Scott in Tommy's room. Both Doctor Joe and Gail knew that this would be the most difficult day of all - for Tommy. But, it was also going to be a painful day for everyone else, including them. This was the day that they would remove the bandages and show Tommy, and then the rest of the world his face. Yes, it was going to be a very painful day indeed.

As he approached the door, Doctor Jankowski stopped for a moment. Gail stopped and turned to look at him. He closed his eyes for a moment and took a very deep breath. Gail touched his arm gently and said soothingly, "Joe, you did the best you could and you are the best. We'll keep doing skin grafts until we get his face back."

He turned to look at her with an awful sadness in his eyes. Like a blow to his face, he winced at her words and suddenly realized the weight he was about to put on this little boy's shoulders. "No, Gail, I'm afraid, he'll never have his face back...he's beyond my abilities to repair him. What he needs is a miracle...but thanks."

"Hello, Ace. How are the Chocomonsters?" Doctor Joe asked. He waved weakly to Joanna and Scott Flagg. They appeared uncomfortable to the doctor. They also knew that it was going to be a tough morning.

"Gone," Tommy said sullenly.

"Oh, well. How would you like to eat your next bowl of Chocomonsters at home?" Doctor Joe asked trying to be upbeat, more for himself than anyone else.

"You mean, I can go home?" Tommy suddenly recovered from the loss of his favorite cereal.

"Yup, that's what I'm saying, Ace. You're goin' home. It's about time, don't you think? And besides, isn't it about time for spring training?"

Without waiting for an answer, Doctor Jankowski said more seriously now as he sat at the side of the bed, "Tommy, we've gone as far as we can go for the moment. You need to go home, Tommy. You need to be with your folks here; and get some rest; go back to school. You know, get back to normal." In his heart, however, the doctor knew that this little boy's life was going to be anything but normal - for the rest of his life.

Doctor Jankowski continued, "Tommy, unfortunately, it's not over for you. Yea, you can go home for a while, but I'm afraid that we're going to be doing more of those skin grafts; you know, the kind we did the other day. Are you ready for those?

"Yes," Tommy said, sensing Doctor Joe's sudden seriousness.

Doctor Joe looked deeply into Tommy's eyes. This would be the last and probably the most difficult question he would be asking this ten year old to confront. He took a deep breath which everyone in the room noticed and then said, "Tommy, there's one last thing before I let you out. I can take off the bandages so you can see what you look like, or we can just wait until your next visit. What do you think?"

Everything was going so well. What could be the harm? Hadn't Doctor Joe saved him; made him well. He could see. He got him the Chocomonsters. Besides, how bad could it really be? You know moms and dads; they always want to protect you from something. You know, like, Tommy, it's really cold, or it's really hot; be careful - it's really dangerous. How bad could it be? A part of him was curious; he wanted to know the truth. He had to know what he looked like before he left the hospital and saw his friends. But there was something in Doctor Joe's face; in his voice; in the way that he called him "Tommy" instead of "Ace", the name he had become accustomed to as Doctor Joe's trademark. His Mom and Dad also looked very serious; they hadn't said a word. Suddenly, he was unsure. Suddenly, he had a feeling in the pit of his stomach that this time, he wasn't going to like what he heard. But still, he had to go through with it; he had to know. There was a long pause. No one spoke. All eyes were on Tommy.

"OK, Doctor Joe. Is it going to hurt?"

"No, Tommy, it shouldn't hurt," Doctor Joe said. But how do you tell a ten year old about emotional pain; about the pain when he sees himself scarred and deformed for life and probably beyond anybody's power to heal him, to bring him back to normal.

"Well, Tommy, if you're ready, we'll take off your bandages for a moment, so you can see yourself. Before I do, Tommy, I want you to know that it will probably look bad to you. You won't look like you did before your face was burned. You've got scars and your face and neck are still very raw from the burns. And that's not all. You've lost most of your hair, although that will grow back in a matter of a few weeks? We've done everything we can thus far, Tommy. I'm not going to give up on trying to get you back to normal. The rest of it is up to you...Ready?"

"I'm ready," Tommy said but he knew he wasn't. Maybe, he should put this off. His mother and father were now on opposite sides of the bed and each took one of his hands. He looked at them questioningly. He could see their faces taut and tense. They were also readying themselves for the worst. Gail was standing at the foot of the bed looking at him; no, watching him, no, standing by ready to help in some way he did not understand. She had a mirror in her hand. Everyone went quiet. He could feel the tension mounting in the room. The doctor approached him. Tommy knew by the hard, pained expression on Doctor Joe's face that this was all wrong; that it was going to hurt. *Maybe, I really don't want to do this now*...Doctor Jankowski sensed Tommy's growing trepidation but it was too late. Before Tommy could change his mind and say, "*No. Stop! I changed my mind*", the doctor started taking off the bandages.

Tommy's body went stiff with tension. He began squeezing his parents' hands harder and harder. His father put a hand on Tommy's chest; his mother rubbed his arm. "It's all right, Tommy, it's going to be all right. We're here and we love you," his mother said trying to soothe him. Tommy's eyes changed from those of a ten year old boy to those of a wild animal suddenly caged. His eyes darted from person to person; then to the window; then to the mirror in Gail's hand. Then back to the doctor who had the look of stone. His eyes were now crazed with terror. Tommy's chest began to heave; he began to pant. He started to raise his arms and legs, but suddenly felt strong hands holding them in place.

And then the bandages were off...Doctor Joe reached for the mirror

Joanna and Scott Flagg saw their little boy's face. Joanna gasped and tried to stifle a scream but the muted sound came out; Scott groaned audibly. Tears of agony welled up in his eyes. He remembered the horror of seeing his son in the bus, and now this. *Oh, God, my Tommy!*

Doctor Jankowski was saying to Tommy, "Now, Tommy, this will look worse than it probably is but...."

and mumbled something else as he reached for the mirror and brought it slowly in front of Tommy.

For an instant, Tommy stared in the mirror, not comprehending that he was looking in a mirror. He saw some freakish image of ...*something* in the mirror. It wasn't human. For a moment, he forgot that he was holding a mirror. This was some ghoulish picture that Doctor Joe wanted him to see, so that he could say, "You see, Tommy, that's a really bad burn, but not in your case...you look like this." For an instant he waited for Doctor Joe to pass him the real mirror.

And then...then it came crashing down on him. He **was** looking into the mirror...and, *Oh my God, it's me!*

Nothing...no one could have prepared him for what he saw. It couldn't be explained away with soothing and comforting words. This...this...*thing* was him - Tommy Flagg. He was afraid of his own reflection!

He lashed at the mirror that went crashing to the floor, shattering. And then he screamed. It didn't come from his lungs. It came from Tommy's soul. He howled like a wounded dog. He thrashed his arms and his legs; whipping his head from side to side trying somehow to shake the image from his mind. It was an image he could never conjure up even in his worst nightmare. Not so long as he lived would he forget that moment. It was his new face; no, it was a death mask.

His screams brought the other nurses rushing into the room. Doctor Jankowski raised his hand to stop them from doing anything. His voice was hard, "Leave him alone; there's no other way right now. Let him cry; let him grieve alone."

The room was now filled with nurses, and orderlies who could only stand by helplessly at the little boy whom they had come to know and care over these weeks and watch as he struggled with a horrifying reality. Joanna and Scott stared in horror at both Tommy's face and his agony. They held his hands tightly. Everyone waited.

Slowly, Tommy's agonizing cries began to subside. It took more energy than he had then to continue. His crying turned to a soft whimper. The shock, horror and confrontation with his reflection in the mirror had exhausted Tommy. He drifted off into a fitful sleep. For the remainder of the day, he would cry out in his sleep, his little body would shake convulsively, then he would cry and fall back to sleep.

"Let him sleep," Doctor Jankowski ordered. He turned to Joanna and Scott. "Are you all right?" he asked softly.

Joanna was dumbstruck. She tried to say something but couldn't get the words out. She tried mouthing the words. She moved her lips but no sounds came out. She reached out for Scott; she needed him now. But before she could reach Scott's hand, her arm went limp, and she slumped over on to Tommy's bed.

CHAPTER 11

"No, I'm not going. I look like a monster. They'll laugh at me," Tommy said grimly.

"Tommy, they're your friends. They all know what happened. Of course, they'll understand. They won't laugh." His mother was trying to assure him ever since they left the hospital a week ago, but it was no use. Tommy was not about to return to school.

His mother tried a different approach: "Tommy, what about having some of your friends come over for a visit. I'm sure you'll want to see Mark. He's your best friend. It will just be like every other..."

"No! No, I don't want to see Mark, not anybody...ever."

"OK, Tommy. All right. I understand. But you have to get ready now. We have to go see Doctor Joe."

"Why does it have to be during the day? Why not at night? Why can't he come here?" Tommy said defiantly to his mother.

"Tommy, please. We have to go to see Doctor Joe. We need to change your bandages; and to schedule your next skin graft," Joanna Flagg said more as a plea.

"Why? Why do we have to go to see **_him_**. He can't do anything for me. He didn't when I was in the hospital. Is he going to make me look the way I did before the accident? No. I'm ugly. You know it; he knows it; everyone knows it. I'm not going; not now; not ever. I'm not ever going out of this house."

Doctor Jankowski and Gail came to the house for the next several weeks in order to change Tommy's dressings.

After one particularly tense visit by Doctor Jankowski, a visit where Tommy would not even say hello to either Doctor Joe or to Gail Franklin, Joanna Flagg asked, "Doctor, what do you think? He's hurting so much. I can't get him to go out, not even in the garden. He won't have anyone of his friends over here. I don't know what to do." Joanna was confused and very frustrated. She looked pale and worn.

"Mrs. Flagg…Joanna, we can't push him. Physically, he's capable of going back to school now. Emotionally…I just don't know. I don't think anyone knows. But I do know, it won't do any good to force him."

For the next three weeks, Tommy remained at home. Most of the time he barricaded himself in his room. He refused repeated entreaties from his mother to come to the kitchen table for his meals, demanding rather that his meals be brought to his room.

Lately, he had even started to draw the curtains in his room so that he was in darkness for most of the day. And for most of the day, he sat glumly in front of the small television his parents had put in his room when he came home from the hospital. He sat watching early morning cartoons, followed by an endless stream of monster movie reruns and baseball games. He wasn't really watching, though; he just stared into the screen.

He had stopped laughing.

Another week. All the bandages were off by now and the redness and swelling had all but disappeared leaving his face a pale pink. But, the scars, particularly on his face were extensive. There were thick raised lines, kris crossing on his cheeks and forehead. His left ear was also scarred from the surgery. The hair on his head and eyebrows was growing back slowly.

His mother decided that she would try once more to reach her son. The door to his room was ajar and she could see him sitting in the dark in front of the TV. The glow of the TV twisted the lines on his face exaggerating the scars.

"Tommy, may I come in?" his mother asked softly.

He wasn't really watching TV; not even listening really.

"Sure, Mom," he sighed as if it were an effort because he knew what she was going to say. "Come in."

"Tommy,... honey," she was struggling, "You can't ..."

He cut her off, "Yes, I can. Yes, I can stay here forever."

"No, Tommy, you can't do this to yourself. I know, Tommy, it looks bad, but you can't just hide in this room for the rest of your life. You have to start again.

And so it went for yet another week. Tommy was intractable; and his mother, Joanna was equally determined to see her son take the first step. Neither would budge.

The days passed slowly. It seemed that the snow had refused to melt, keeping Spring at bay. But from time to time the face of Spring did peek from behind the snow clouds. It was Monday, and it was a glorious day! The snow glistened briefly in the warming sun and then was turned into droplets of water, forming little pools on the path to the street. As Tommy peeked through the curtains, he actually heard birds chirping. And then he heard the best sound of all. It was Mark riding his bicycle with the other kids on the slush covered road. He could here them laughing.

"Race ya," Mark called out.

Immediately, each of them stood up on his bike, and began to pedal furiously, skidding and sliding as they tried to retain control in the icy mush. They laughed and taunted one another. Each biker answered the call. With shouts of encouragement and legs pumping, they were off!

No one even looked in the direction of Tommy's house.

He watched them pedal off in the distance. He strained to hear every word...and then they disappeared over the hill. He drew the curtain and as he turned to return to his beanbag chair in front of the television, he saw his mother standing at his door. He looked at her for a very long time. Neither of them said a word. Joanna Flagg waited; she knew that his heart was aching to be out there with his friends but she couldn't force it any longer. The decision had to be Tommy's.

He took in a deep almost painful breath, and sighed, "OK, Mom. I'll try, but if anyone laughs, I'm never going back."

She opened her arms to him and said, "Oh, Tommy, I'm so proud of you. I know you can do it. You're very brave. I know it's going to be all right."

CHAPTER 12

Scott and Joanna drove Tommy to school the next morning. His mother wanted to walk him to his class but Tommy insisted that he was ready to go alone.

Tommy got out of the car and walked into the corridor. It was a cool, dark hallway and very quiet. It had the distinctive smell of the disinfectant that was used to clean the floor. He could hear his footsteps echoing off the walls. The doors to each of the classrooms were closed. All of the kids were now in their homeroom classes settling in for another day. He prayed that no one would see him. As he walked along the corridor, he could see several of his friends in other classes. They were laughing and joking with one another, but he couldn't hear their voices. The hallway suddenly became even quieter by the time he reached the door of his class. He could see in the window. He saw their happy faces; smiling and apparently talking excitedly with one another. But because the door was closed, he couldn't hear a sound. All he saw was their lips moving. As he stood there in the ghostly quiet hall, he thought he could hear his own heart beating. He pulled the cap further down over his head - his hair hadn't quite grown back in. He looked like a "fuzzy butt head" he told his mother.

His mouth was very dry and he struggled to take several deep swallows, but nothing was going to help. He was scared. *"How would they react?"* he wondered. *"Would they laugh; or would they cry. Would they just treat him like Tommy...ace pitcher, or an ugly cripple?"*

He took a deep breath, held it and turned the doorknob. He stepped in.

The room fell silent immediately. There were a few gasps. He thought he heard someone say, "Who's that?"

His teacher, Mrs. Germaine, rushed over to him from her desk and gave him a hug. "Welcome back, Tommy. We've missed you."

Even though Mrs. Germaine had told the class about Tommy's injury and tried to make them understand how Tommy might be feeling, she could not prepare them for what they saw.

With her arm still wrapped around Tommy, she said to the group, "Well, class, what do you say? Let's all welcome Tommy back. How about we clap our hands and shout, 'Welcome back Tommy!' We love you."

But nothing – not a sound. Just stunned silence.

Suddenly, one of the girls, Melanie Jameson, started to cry. Through her tears, she was stammered, "He's...he's so...ugly. Poor Tommy." Mark Lowell, Tommy's best friend, went over to Tommy, and just stood there. He couldn't utter a word so great was his shock. Someone in the back of the room muttered

"...freaky." Mrs. Germaine tried to speak but it was too late. Melanie asked to leave the room and a few of the other kids did the same. Mark seemed to be riveted to his spot. Mrs. Germaine felt helpless and Tommy just stood there with eyes cast down, shattered.

Mrs. Germaine, holding Tommy tightly to her side, glared at the class. Through tight lips and a hard edge in her voice said slowly, and deliberately, emphasizing each word, "Class, you all know the terrible accident and suffering that Tommy has been through. I think that we as his friends and classmates can help him through this difficult time". They felt as if her cold glance was meant for each of one of them. Then she finished with "Don't you agree?"

She motioned to Tommy take his usual seat in the third row, third seat.

With a final hard stare at the class, she said, "OK, class, let's begin."

Each class Tommy went to was the same: the same shocked expressions; the same stunned silence; the same whispered comments with words overheard like, "ugly", "gross", "snake face". He felt more like a circus animal; like a creature behind a glass cage, stared at, pitied or ridiculed. He wasn't any longer Tommy Flagg, ten-year-old ace baseball pitcher in Pine Creek School.

Tommy elected to eat his lunch in one of the classrooms. He couldn't bear the thought of going into the cafeteria. It just meant more comments; more shocked stares; and teachers with those sappy, puppy dog looks on their faces which were supposed to convey to everyone that everything was normal. *Sure, normal. My face is burned, and scarred. It's gross and ugly. Sure, everything is great. I just want to get out of here; and go home.*

He ate his lunch alone. No one came in to sit with him.

After what seemed an eternity, the school bell rang to signal that the day was mercifully over for Tommy. He was the last to leave the classroom. It seemed that everyone just wanted to get out of there as much as he did. No one wanted to be seen walking with *him*. He pulled his cap low over his face. Perhaps, he could make it out the side door without anymore of the kids noticing. But Tommy was about to endure one final agony.

As he walked down the corridor toward the door to meet his parents, he kept close to the walls hiding in the dim hallway light. He hoped that in the usual chaos and bedlam in the corridor at the end of the school day, he would go unnoticed. But they caught sight of him, and then it went dead quiet. Kids just stared at him as he walked by, hunched over, facing the wall as he walked. The bill of his cap nearly covered his eyes. It was obvious to the kids that he was hiding his face. By this time, everyone had heard the rumors about his horrific facial injuries. All conversation seemed to hang frozen in the air; no slamming of locker doors: no sneakers being tossed around; no shoving to be first out the door and on the bus. Silence. Deafening silence - and the stares.

Tommy turned and saw what he felt were a thousand eyes just staring blankly, stupidly. He stood there staring back at them, the anger growing like a fire in a furnace. He stepped forward as if in slow motion, drew his shoulder back and in doing so seemed to grow beyond his small fame. He slowly lifted his cap and faced them for one last time. His eyes burned like coals and slowly, so slowly, his voice venomous with barely suppressed rage, he almost hissed when he spoke: "I... hate...you."

He quickly turned and bolted out of the door. He couldn't let them see that he had tears in his eyes, but he burned with anger and resentment. *Never again. I'll never go back there.*

"Well, Tommy, how did it go?" his father asked cheerily as Tommy climbed in alongside his mother on the passenger side. He didn't answer. He couldn't answer. He buried his face in his mother's shoulder and cried and cried all the way home. And when he couldn't cry any longer, his little body was wracked with sobs too large for a ten year old to have to endure.

CHAPTER 13

After arriving home, Tommy went without a word directly to his room. He drew the curtains and sat at the edge of his bed. His parents followed him in. Through tears and a breaking heart, he told his parents what had happened earlier that day in school. He kept shaking his head, saying over and over, "Why...why, me. I was a good boy, wasn't I, Mom. Why did God make this happen to me?" His mother listened quietly. There was nothing to say. Certainly, nothing that she could say now would make it any better. She was feeling her own pain of guilt for having pushed Tommy to go back to school.

Tommy refused to come out of his room later that evening for dinner. She brought him his favorite dinner - hamburger and French fries with the bottle of ketchup on the side. But it went cold. He just sat in the darkness of his room. To Tommy, the darkness was now the only sanctuary, the only friend he had. Except for his Mom and Dad, he never wanted to be seen by anyone ever again.

Scott and Joanna Flagg had left Tommy to his own thoughts for the remainder of the evening. On the way to bed, they came into his room and turned on the small table lamp on Tommy's desk. Joanna sat beside Tommy and put her arm around his shoulder. Tommy looked over at his father, and with a mixture of sadness and anger in his voice, he said, "Dad, you should've just let me die. Look at me, Dad, just look at me. No one can help me. I'll be like this forever. I'm better off dead." And with that Tommy tore himself away from his mother's arms. Joanna Flagg started to say something, but Scott put his hand on her arm and shook his head as if to say, "Leave him be."

It was later that night when something awakened Tommy. He could hear sounds of people in his bad dream, the sounds of the kids screaming as the bus kept falling...and falling. Their screams filled his head. And then, the screams were real. No, not screams but voices, loud voices, angry voices. This was not a dream, this was real. He could hear the angry voices and they were voices that he recognized. It was his Mom and Dad. They were arguing. He couldn't make out the words, just the loud voices.

He got out of bed and tiptoed out of his room into the hallway. The voices were more distinct and he thought he could hear his name mentioned once or twice. He was frightened. He had never heard his parents arguing like this before. Oh, yea, they had their quarrels, mostly about Scott "procrastinating" whatever that meant. But this sounded different. These were really angry voices.

Tommy got down on his hands and knees and in the darkness of the corridor crawled toward the light coming from under their bedroom door. Something inside of him did not want to hear what was being said. He knew somehow he was going to regret this, but something else told him that he had to because he was involved. After all, he did hear his name mentioned. He reached the door and sat up with his back against the wall. He drew up his knees to his chest and wrapped his arms around them to listen to the angry voices:

"You're too protective, Scott...he has to go back to school."

"No, Joanna. He's not ready. Leave him be for awhile. Why are you pushing him...? What are you trying to do? Don't you understand? He's in pain?"

"We can get help for him...

"What kind of help, a shrink? Why do you think that's always the answer?

"No, I don't think it's always the answer, but in this case..."

"Joanna, this case? This case? This is our son you're talking about...not a case?"

"You're twisting my words. What do **you** want, Scott, do you want us to leave him in his room to languish until he's twenty-one?"

"No, I just think that we should give him some time, Joanna, and some space. You're smothering him."

"Smothering him? Is that what you think? I love him, and I feel his pain as his mother. But that doesn't mean that we should just let him vegetate in his dark room like a mushroom."

"And, do **you** think that a shrink is going to make it easier for him to withstand the cruelty from the kids. Do *you* think that it's going to be easier for him day after day? Is that what you're saying?"

"Well, with the help of the school and the teachers, yes, I think that we can do it, if we all pitch in to help Tommy."

Scott laughed derisively, "Naive, that's what you are, Joanna, naive. Why don't you stop trying to play doctor and for once put yourself in his shoes."

"For once, Scott? For once? And what have I been doing all these weeks? Do you think I have all the answers? Well, I don't. But I do know that if he's ever going to survive emotionally, he's got to go back."

"Joanna, don't you understand? He's in pain. He's going to be the butt of jokes for the rest of his time in this school and probably beyond that. And, yes, maybe for the rest of his life. Kids are cruel because they don't understand. They just react. He needs time, lots of time. Leave him be!

"No, I will not!"

"Who are you to do this to him; to make this decision about what he needs. You don't feel his pain. They're not laughing at you. You're beautiful and will always be. I'm sorry to say this, Joanna, but he's ugly. Joanna, he's ugly."

It hit Tommy like thunder right above his head. *'He's ugly.'* For a moment, he couldn't breathe. His heart began to throb violently, and he forced himself to take deep breaths. *'He's ugly.'* The sound kept ringing in his ears. *'He's ugly.'*

He scrabbled from the door to his own room, got up and ran in. He stood in the dark in the middle of the room, struggling to maintain his balance. **'He's ugly...he's ugly.'** Over and over, the sound of it shrieked in his ears. He couldn't escape it. It stuck to him like a skin rash, like an indelible stain. He started to rub his arms and his scarred face ferociously hoping that it would rub off. But it wouldn't come off.

Then, as if a light had flashed in his eyes, he stopped. He stood there motionless in the darkness for several minutes. No, there was no escape from this. He would look like this for the rest of his life. People laughing at him, staring at him like some freak in a circus. *Doctors, operations, nurses, more doctors, a shrink, kids laughing and staring at me...for the rest of my life.* Why, even his father agreed that he was ugly. He remembered a horror movie he had seen where the poor monster, who really wasn't a monster after all, was forced to live in a dark and cold tower of a castle. Everyone was afraid to look at him. He was ugly too. He had a hunchback, long hair and dragged his leg. Is that what would become of him too? "Tommy, the Ugly Man." He formed the picture of it in his mind.

"No...no," Tommy said out loud. "No, I will not become a monster for everyone to stare at, or laugh at." Then, just as quickly, he stopped shuddering, and a calmness came over him. He knew what he had to do.

Almost without thinking about it, he quickly made his bed, stuffed some things in his backpack, put on his winter jacket and climbed out the window.

He dropped to the ground and heard the crunch of snow under his feet. He stood there for a moment to get his bearings. He looked up into a sharp, clear night sky. A full moon hung in the sky together with a billion stars. For an instant the fields across the road turned into a magical silvery carpet that beckoned him. He took a deep breath and felt a shiver go through his body. He wondered whether it was from the cold or from what he was doing. Yes, he knew what he was doing. He had to go. He didn't belong here anymore. Not to his Mom and Dad, not to his school, not to his friends. He looked up at the window for his parents' room. The light was out. The angry voices had ceased. Yes, it was better this way. Without him, there wouldn't be any arguments. They would miss him, he hoped, but they would soon forget; they had each other. And well, ...they could always have more babies.... ones that didn't look like him.

He turned to walk down the snow-covered path. All he could hear were his boots, "crunch, crunch" breaking the icy stillness. He walked down the path to the road, and then turned to take one last look at his house. It is ...**was** a special place...Hamburgers, Chocomonsters, Mom, Dad, mornings, Christmas...

He stopped himself from thinking any further. It hurt too much. He took a long deep breath of the frosty night air; hunched his shoulders; then forced himself to turn around and walk into the field. As he did so, he felt a lump building in his throat, and his eyes became moist, but he fought the urge to cry.

CHAPTER 14

As he stepped into the field, he felt like he was wading into a lake of molten silver that stretched out in front of him until it poured into the deep night sky. The sound of his boots cracking the top layer of ice filled his ears; each footfall sounding louder than the last, then fading into the blackness above him. With his hands in his pockets, his shoulders hunched up, and the hood on his jacket drawn up, he could have been a ghostly apparition that floated across the field forming a dark and ominous silhouette against the glistening moon. Tommy could hear his breathing as he trudged through the icy field. The vapor from his labored breathing came out in silver rushes against the night sky. He stopped to listen, perhaps even vaguely hoping that he would hear his mother and father, maybe even his friends calling for him to return, *"Come back, Tommy, come back! It's OK, you're not ugly; we love you. It's going to be all right."* Silence. He turned to look back. The house had disappeared behind the last rise. He was alone now, very alone.

He walked on, more slowly now and with more effort as he could feel the land rising beneath him. Without realizing it, he was walking into the hills, toward White Bluff. He had to stop several times to rest. He still hadn't completely recovered from his accident. His legs felt like lead and he was breathing hard. He leaned over and put his hands on his thighs, forcing himself to take slow deep breaths. He watched the steam rhythmically puffing out of his nostrils. He set off again only to stop after several hundred yards of steep terrain. Start and stop for a rest. Progress was measured a few yards at a time. He had now left the field and had entered the dense forest below White Bluff. He could see the top of the Bluff looming above him. It formed a large and shapeless mass that looked like a dense black against the night sky. It reminded him of the forbidding Black Holes he had heard about in his science class. It looked menacing in the darkness but he couldn't help being drawn to it. He felt a strange and irresistible urge to leap into that impenetrable darkness. He decided that would be his destination - not White Bluff, but the Black Hole. He would disappear in the Black Hole. *No one can hurt me there. Maybe there are other kids like me. I'll just be normal.*

Just below the top of the Bluff, the forest abruptly gave way to several hundred feet of shale with massive boulders on either side. He decided to attack the mountain face straight on. From this point on, it was going to be hand over hand. Progress would now be measured a few feet at a time. Tommy struggled over the shale with each step. He kept slipping back, regaining his footing and then slipping back again. Yet, he pressed on. *I wonder what it's going to like to live in a Black Hole. What do you do for food; what do they look like in there? Who's they? What am I thinking? I must be going crazy.*

He pushed himself harder. He missed his step and slide down several feet scraping his hands and face on the loose stones. He lay there spread eagle with his face pressed against the cold shale. He could feel his heart beating, and his burning lungs heaving underneath him. He could smell the damp Earth inches from his nose. He scrabbled to his left where the shale line ended about 30 feet away at enormous boulders. As he worked his way across the steep shale, he slid a few feet further down, frustrating him to the point of rage. He screamed curses out at the night, smashing his fist against the stones which only made him hurt the more. He was now determined to get to the top of White Bluff. *There's no Black Hole, stupid! There's no place to hide.* Then he forced himself to forget everything else, and summoned all his energy to get to the boulders.

With his last ounce of determination, he slipped and slid his way across, and as he did so, sent a cascade of shale down the hill below him in a rumble that filled his head and which he thought could have been heard for miles. He lashed his left arm out and with his fingertips managed to grab a hold on to one of the boulders. *I made it, I made it. I'm going to make it. But where am I going? Forget that. Get to the Bluff. One step at a time.*

Tommy pulled himself up against the boulder and leaned his back against it. His breath came more in gasps. His mouth felt like cotton wool. He licked his lips to moisten them. It didn't help. He was looking out over the forest below him and in the distance the cornfield where he used to live. *Used to live.* That sounded strange, but that's what it was. He could not go back...ever. Beyond the field, the dark sky was blending into to a lighter shade of gray...morning. It was going to be morning soon. *I've been out here all night.* He looked around the boulder. Above him, the Black Hole had disappeared and the gray light had turned the black hole back into White Bluff. He thought of home. *In a little while, Mom and Dad will be getting up to start their day. She would-be making coffee, and he'll be asking her where she had put his boots. "They're on the back porch, dear, just where you put them last night, and every night before that."*

He shook his head violently to rid himself of the warm images. He had to press on. He ached all over. He was covered in bloody and painful scratches. *What difference does it make. I can't look any uglier than I already do.*

Deciding against climbing back onto the shale, he worked his way continuously to his left over and around the boulders. Climbing was somewhat easier now, more so because it was getting lighter. As it was easier, he felt his mind wandering on home, his friends, family, the hospital and his face...his face. It haunted him so. *I'm afraid of my own face. I'm a freak.*

He was so absorbed in those thoughts that he never noticed the wetness on the stones. The chill of the night was being warmed by the coming morning leaving a thin layer of moisture covering the earth. His hands weren't getting a good grip, and he began to lose his footing, but again, he didn't notice. He kept seeing his face in front of him – the scars that would be with him for the rest of his life. He closed his eyes tightly hoping that would make face go away, but he couldn't. And then he could no longer hold it in. For the entire night, he had struggled with the cold, the icy field, the shale, and the boulders. But he couldn't fight off his own demons.

As he struggled, slipped and slid, tears welled into his eyes, and he cried aloud, **"Why?...why? Why me? What am I going to do? Not like this for the rest of my life. I just can't."**

He stopped absentmindedly several times to wipe the streaming tears with his jacket sleeve. Over and over, he asked himself the same questions: *"Why?...why? Why me?. What am I going to do? Not like this for the rest of my life. I just can't.*

And then he slipped.

It happened so quickly. First he was standing up, and then he was falling. Suddenly, time seemed to slow down. It felt as if he were settling down in a bowl of Jell-O. He remembered the feeling from the last time. Yes, in the bus as it tumbled down the ravine. He could feel that his body was hitting the rocks; but he really didn't feel the pain. This slow motion even slowed the pain from reaching him. He had no idea how long he had been rolling, tumbling and falling. Somewhere deep inside him, it didn't hurt anymore. He was almost glad of it.

Maybe, I'm falling in the Black Hole. Now the pain will go. And I'll just go away too.

The falling stopped just as Tommy's head hit a stone. And then everything went black. His breathing slowed; and a small smile formed on his lips. *I made it...I made it...the Black Hole.... Good-bye, mom. I love you.*

CHAPTER 15

Perhaps, it was a premonition. Mothers are like that, you know. Perhaps, it was that she didn't hear his restless murmurings in his sleep; or his screams from bad dreams ever since the accident. Yes, there was something wrong, very wrong. She had been asleep when the feelings interrupted her dreams and she awakened with the feeling, no a dread. Joanna Flagg nearly jumped out of the bed. Her husband, Scott, felt the jarring motion, "Wha, ...whas the matter, Joanna," Scott said sleepily.

"It's Tommy. Something's wrong...". Her voice trailed off as she ran naked to Tommy's room. She saw that the door was shut. It was never shut. Tommy liked the idea of having the door open, particularly when he was having bad dreams. Now she was certain. She opened the door and called into the darkness, "Tommy!"

No response. She felt the cold from the open window before she wheeled around to see it. In a flash she knew. "Oh, my God. Tommy!" She ran to the partially opened window and screamed out Tommy's name, again and again, but she knew that it was futile. She knew that he was long gone and that something bad had happened. It was the same feeling she got the last time. The time when the bus...She couldn't bear to think about it. *Oh, not again. Tommy, Tommy. Not again.*

Scott came stumbling in. He saw the empty bed and his wife sitting on the edge of Tommy's bed with his pillow pressed against her breasts, sobbing, "Oh, no. Tommy, my poor Tommy. What have we done. Oh, my God, what have we done?"

Scott ran out of the room, leaving Joanna to her tears. There was no time to lose. Within minutes, Scott had his clothes on and was out in the garden looking for something, anything which could tell him where Tommy had gone. The gray morning light was just beginning to fill in the dark shadows remaining from the night, so he almost missed them. But then he saw the footprints. He ran after them, out of the garden, across the road and into the field. The tracks were straight and true. They told Scott that Tommy was determined when he left, determined to go. *But where? Where? Where have you gone, Tommy.*

Scott started to run into the field. Then stopped. *No this isn't the way. He could be anywhere. The sheriff. That's it, the sheriff. We need manpower, helicopters. We have got to find him. He's out there somewhere.*

His eyes scanned the horizon. The fields went on for miles in every direction. He could see the hills and White Bluff, a bluish green slash on the horizon off to his right. He turned around and ran back to the house. Joanna was already dressed and waiting by the door.

"Joanna, I found his tracks. They lead into the field. You call the Sheriff, and I'll get the truck. I'll meet you out front. He couldn't have got that far." But he knew he was lying to her. Tommy could be miles into the field in any direction. He could have fallen in any one of several gullies with streams running through them; or he could have headed into the hills, toward White Bluff. But he knew that every moment they delayed meant that the tracks would be more difficult to follow.

"Hurry, Joanna, we gotta get out there before the sun comes up and melts those tracks."

CHAPTER 16

He was aware first that he wasn't dead, or at least he thought so. He remembered falling. Yes, he was falling into the Black Hole. There was no pain, just falling. *Where am I now. Is this the Black Hole. No, there's no Black Hole. That was White Bluff. Then where am I?*

Tommy was afraid to open his eyes. So, he concentrated on his face. He pursed his lips and wrinkled his scarred forehead for starters. Next, he tried to wiggle his fingers and toes, but he couldn't. He felt a numbness where his fingers and toes should be. Slowly he was becoming aware of something else. Pain. The pain was not in any one place but it seemed to be a fire which was building and spreading wider and wider. But yet, it was strange, because he felt something else. He felt warm. It was as if he were near a camp fire. But that wasn't possible. He hadn't built a fire and all he could now begin to remember was slipping and falling. He was afraid of the warm feeling. Maybe it was blood. His mom had told him that humans are warm blooded. But that wasn't it. A campfire? It really shouldn't be there. He still hadn't opened his eyes. Perhaps, if he kept them shut a little longer, it would go away. *I have got to open my eyes and see. Maybe someone found me and has built a fire to keep me warm. Or, maybe, it's a monster whose about to have me for breakfast.* He willed his eyes to open. Slowly, just a slit at first, then all the way. He turned his head left to right and then rolled his eyes up and down.

The entire area was bathed in a golden yellow light, but there was no fire or other lights that he could see. He tried but his body hurt so that he was unable to move. It was still warm. Not uncomfortable, just right as a matter of fact. He looked up and could see the sky through the branches. *How far did I fall?* It was still early morning. The sky above was a light gray, and all but the brightest stars were gone for the day. But yet, the light surrounding him was so bright, too bright for this time of morning. Now he could feel the pain striking him with its full fury. He cried out, then howled sounding more like a young wolf than a young boy. His eyes widened as he struggled to move away from the pain rather than from a desire to see his surroundings. And as he did so, from the corner of eye, he caught the sight of something...his reflection.

Reflection?

No, that can't be. How could that be my reflection. There's no mirror, but there it is, it's my reflection, or at least it's someone or something that looks like me. Wait! It's not one reflection. It's TWO! What..?.

Slowly, he put a swollen hand to his forehead, "Ugh," he moaned aloud. His head hurt and his vision was blurry. He tried squinting his eyes in an effort to refocus, but the blurriness was still there and so were the two ...yes, two people. No, he thought to himself, he wasn't seeing double.   And they definitely were not his reflections! But yet, they looked something like he him. Maybe, he **did** fall into a Black Hole and maybe all the people looked like he did after accidents. His reflections, they, or whatever, didn't move. They were just looking at him. *They? Looking? No, it can't be. I'm seeing things.* They were surrounded in the same light, but Tommy couldn't see a fire. He could feel the warmth, and at least that made him feel better, although he still couldn't feel his fingers and toes.

An ominous thought struck him. He frowned and said aloud, "Maybe, I'm really dead. Maybe this is what it feels like to die."

Then, the strangest thing happened. He heard...or thought he heard a voice: *"No, you're not dead, but if we don't get you some help, I'm afraid you are going to die."*

Tommy looked in the direction of both his reflections, ...them, or whatever. Tommy knew he heard it. *They did say, "No, you're not dead, but if we don't get you some help, I'm afraid you are going to die."*

But they were still staring at him. Their lips weren't moving, but yet he heard something! How?...Who was speaking?

Tommy shook his head. The fall was worse than he thought. First he was seeing things, now he was hearing things. "What did you say?" Tommy asked. *Oh, my God, now I'm talking to these things!*

"Yes, *Tommy, you heard us. You really should not be out here in this cold.*"

"But, how do you know my name...and who, who are you...you sorta, well, look almost like me...but your lips aren't...", came pouring out of Tommy, but before he could finish...

"*We know who you are, Tommy, and we also know what happened to you and that you are very seriously injured. Now, why don't you let us help you? There's nothing to be afraid of.*"

And as Tommy blurted out, "See, your lips **aren't** moving," he felt himself being lifted ever so gently off the icy ground...but they weren't holding him. He was floating! He hadn't learned how to swim, and it frightened him. Instinctively, his arms and legs started to flail, and he gasped with the pain from his injuries, struggling to hold on to something. He screamed, "Who...what ...are you doing...who are you?"

It's all right, Tommy, we're trying to help. Just think of us as your secret friends, OK?

For the first time since opening his eyes, he took a closer look at these two reflections, things, whatever. It struck him that they did look a bit like him. Well, sort of. They were short – about his height, he guessed - and slight, almost fragile looking. They didn't have any hair. He still had bald spots on his head. Their faces looked like they both had an accident too, but they didn't have any scars or welts. Their skin was smooth unlike his. Their eyes were round and dark – something like his eyes.

Where there should have been a mouth with lips, there was a little pucker instead, like a little baby giving you a kiss; or the after effects from sucking on a lemon – something he did too when his mom made creamed spinach. He couldn't tell if they were naked. Their bodies were covered in the same smooth skin that made up their faces. *Maybe*, he thought, *they were wearing white sheets like Halloween ghosts.* As he looked down at the ground passing about two feet underneath him, he thought of what they just said. *"Just think of us as your secret friends, OK?"*

Turning to the one on his right he said, "Well, OK, but you're not going to kill me and eat me, are you?" Without waiting for an answer, Tommy could not help but think to himself, *No, somehow, I don't think so. I feel warm inside. Too many monster movies, I guess.*

"You're right, Tommy, too many monster movies."

It was strange Tommy thought. *They can hear me, and they're talking to me, but I don't see his mouth, or whatever you call it, moving.* Tommy looked down as they glided slowly and effortlessly over the boulders it had taken him hours to climb. He instinctively reached out for one of his escorts as they passed over a large boulder leaving about a drop of twenty feet below. But then just as suddenly, he felt a calmness come over him. He turned to his escort on the left who looked at him and nodded slowly. He took a deep breath and closed his eyes. It was better not to look down, up... or even sideways.

After a few moments, Tommy could no longer contain his growing panic, "OK, if you're not going to kill me, or eat me, then where are we going?" He looked cautiously at each of them as they floated alongside him. The reflection, thing or whatever on the right looked at Tommy, *We're going to take you where it's safe, and warm. I think parts of you are frozen.* Tommy "heard" but again he noticed that the thing's mouth never changed from the pucker look. "You mean 'ugly' don't you," Tommy hissed. "You're just like the rest." He turned away in disgust.

"No, Tommy. One, I think you've got what your people call 'frostbite'; and two, you're not ugly."

Tommy did not hear. Rather he felt their thoughts entering his body. *Not ugly. They said I'm not ugly.* Almost in response, but more to himself, he asked, "But then who are you and why do we look so much alike, well, sort of?" Tommy looked at each one of them and they looked back at them. And, to his surprise, he understood what they were...thinking. For some reason, Tommy turned to the right. He felt that the thing on the right was addressing him...and he was right. *"My name is Sorgo; and my companion's name is Glefon; and we don't understand either why you look like us, "sort of," but we are going to find out.*

Tommy had not noticed that they had left the rock-strewn face of White Bluff. Suddenly, he noticed that there was no sky. It was morning, and he should have been able to see the sunlight filtering into the green forest. Instead, the woods appeared darker. In fact, Tommy could no longer make out the outline of any trees.

It was growing darker and darker. Then there was no light beyond the golden yellow glow that surrounded him and his two traveling companions. Beyond, there was an impenetrable blackness that sent shivers up his back. *Where are we?* he thought.

"You're safe now, Tommy. We're home," Sorgo communicated as Tommy turned to his companion on the right with a questioning look on his face.

Just then Tommy realised that he had communicated to Sorgo without speaking. He was about to feel very confused, but when he looked at Sorgo who was also looking at him, he felt a wave of warmth and calm come over him. And for the first time, he didn't feel scared. Maybe the Black Hole wasn't such a bad a place after all.

CHAPTER 17

"He's gone Joanna. He's just disappeared. It looks like he made it to the ravine. You know, the one where he had his accident. No, there are no animal tracks. No, no we're certain.   An animal didn't carry him off.   I don't understand it either. We'll keep looking. We'll find him. I promise." Scott handed the mobile phone back to the Sheriff Kanter.

"It's the damnedest thing, Scott," the Sheriff said shaking his head in disbelief. "He left tracks from the house to this spot as clear as a coyote on the prowl, but then nothing. It's just as if he vanished in thin air. How?"

As he looked around him, Scott scowled and shook his head, "Sheriff, I wish I knew. I wish I knew."

Sheriff Kanter called out to the other members of the tracking party, "OK, boys, this is as far as we go tonight. We'll make camp here and start first thing in the morning. OK with you, Scott?"

Scott sighed deeply, knowing that after ten straight hours of trekking over ice covered terrain everyone in the search party was exhausted. They looked at him waiting for him to decide. After all it was his son and they were his friends and neighbors. And if he asked, they were prepared to carry on through the night. He would have done the same for them. "Yea, Sheriff. Let's call it a night."

Sheriff Kanter put his arm on Scott's shoulder and said softly, "I know it looks bad, Scott, but don't give up hope. We'll find him. We'll find him."

CHAPTER 18

Outside of the bubble of light, there was absolutely nothing. Tommy strained his eyes to see where they were taking him. A landmark. He looked for the White Bluff, the fields. Nothing. No light, no trees. Just absolute blackness. "Where are we; where are you taking me," Tommy asked, his voice shaking with fear. A wave of calm started to come over him, but he resisted it. He was afraid. "I want to go home," Tommy called out plaintively.

Just then, the bubble stopped. *"Here we are, Tommy,"* as Tommy turned to Sorgo. He could not tell whether he was rising or falling. Suddenly, it went from the darkness of night into a well-lit high domed chamber. Just as quickly, the bubbles around Sorgo and Glefon disappeared, but he noticed that there was still a glow around himself. By now, Tommy knew that he didn't have to speak to make himself understood, but he decided that he had to speak out loud anyway, if nothing else for the effect. "Sorgo, where are we. What are you going to do with me, and why can't I go home?" His voice sounded like a low rumble of thunder as it echoed in the chamber.

Glefon responded matter of factly by sending a thought which really didn't help and only increased Tommy's apprehension, *"Tommy, you are in the Atmospheric*

Transition Chamber. The bubble of light, as you call it provides you with your air so that you can breathe. It won't hurt." Sorgo could feel Tommy's growing fear and agitation, and then added, *"Don't worry, Tommy; everything will be fine."* It didn't help Tommy at all.

Tommy looked around him. He was standing in a very long and narrow room. It was so long in fact that the room faded into darkness. He turned around to look behind him, but couldn't tell where he had come from because the other end also melted away. It was more like a wide corridor that seemed to go on forever in each direction. The light came from somewhere high above him. Tommy noticed too that there were no chairs, tables or anything else for that matter to indicate where he was - or with whom. Perhaps the feature that struck him most of all were the walls. There were no windows, doorknobs, or handles. This wasn't like anything he had ever seen on Star Trek. Yes, he got the feeling that there were definitely walls out there, but they appeared to Tommy's eyes to be seamless and, well, formless...and they were black, but not just black. It was so black that it almost appeared to be the blackness of empty space. He felt as if he leaned on it, he would fall through.

From the left side of the chamber, a narrow, pencil thin red line suddenly materialized from the floor and shot up several feet. It remained motionless for only a second and then began moving from side to side as if it were scanning from left to right. From the black space across which the red light had traveled, three of these reflections, things or whatever emerged and came toward him in a single file. They all looked the same, yes, something like himself, well, sort of. And dressed, or undressed, the same as Sorgo and Glefon. The three stopped in front of him and for a very long moment just looked at him. Tommy felt like they were studying him. He studied them in return. No, it wasn't an identical match, of course, but there was a resemblance between him and them, but still, their skin was smooth - his was rough and ... He almost thought "scaly". He remembered the remarks of the kids in his class, and then quickly drove the thought away. *How do they tell each other apart*, he thought, but then he realized that everyone knew what he was just thinking. He was going to have to be more careful. Tommy felt embarrassed and a little stupid. *Of course, they can tell each other apart. Otherwise, how would they know who the boys are and who the girls are.*

Tommy's thoughts were interrupted when he felt something. Well, it wasn't feeling actually. He just knew what someone was saying or, rather thinking. This was all very confusing.

"Yes, I guess you could put it that way. We can distinguish each other quite easily. I am Commander Thren. This is my first officer Arnul; and the medical officer, Sharma."

"I'm sorry, sir, I didn't mean...," Tommy mumbled the rest to himself.

"It's quite all right. Now, I understand from Sorgo and Glefon that they found someone who looks like us. And, well, I guess, you

do. At least, I can understand why they felt that way. Tommy, let me assure you that they weren't trying to harm you by bringing you here. Sorgo and Glefon were on routine duty when they came upon you. They also reported that you fell and that you have injuries from your cold weather as well as injuries from your fall. They only wanted to help. Would you like us to help? You can refuse, of course, and I will see to it that you are returned to your people."

"You mean, I can go?" Tommy said, but really knowing what the answer would be.

"Of course, Tommy. We wouldn't hold you here against your will." Commander Thren communicated to Tommy who not only felt what was being said but was starting to feel that the Commander and all these strange people meant him no harm.

Tommy stood there at the same height as the Commander. He looked around at the others who were also the same height. They really did look alike. "I'm sorry, Commander, Sorgo, Glefon if you're hearing this but I really cannot,...but I'll try," he added for good measure. But he knew, he felt that they really did want to help.

"Well, Commander Thren, my hands and feet really hurt, and I have a pain in my side and my leg." Just then, Sharma stepped forward and looked into Tommy's eyes. *"Tommy, I am Sharma. Will you let me examine you."*

"Will it hurt?" Tommy asked hesitantly.

"*No, Tommy, you will feel only a chilling sensation, but that is all,*" Sharma said wordlessly. Tommy looked at Sharma, nodded and in his mind, said, "*OK.*"

Sharma came right up to the tip of Tommy's nose, staring intently into Tommy's face. Sharma's head tilted from side to side as if studying Tommy's face from every angle. Sharma then gently ran a finger over the top of Tommy's head, then his cheeks, mouth and ears. Suddenly, Tommy's eyes widened. At this distance from Sharma's face, he saw something he hadn't noticed before. *They don't have any ears!* There were little holes where the ears should have been.

"*So far so good.*" Tommy thought and projected it to Sharma. "*Wow,*" he thought to himself, "*I'm think-speaking. Cool!*" He intended that Sharma should understand that he was not afraid. That is, until the medical officer reached into a black tube and produced a thick glass rod about a foot in length that suddenly glowed and pulsed a bluish green. Tommy took a step back and started to put his hand up, but just as before, he felt a warmth come over him, a pleasant feeling that made him relax. *How do they do that?* he asked himself. Sharma slowly passed the pulsating wand over the length of Tommy's body, stopping longer at Tommy's face and neck; and then stopping at Tommy's chest and legs. Tommy shivered the way he had on the mountain the night he fell as the rod sent bone-chilling vibrations through him. "*Gees, Sharma, that wasn't a chill, that was freezing.*" Tommy formed the words in his thoughts.

Sharma replied with a terse, "*It was necessary.*"

The doctor looked at the Commander and sent the message that cleared up the mystery - for the visitors at least. "*Commander, Tommy is not one of us. He is a human child from this planet. I will report the Thoron scan results shortly.*" Sharma then turned abruptly and left the chamber.

"*Commander, Tommy is not one of us. He is a human child from this planet.*" Tommy repeated Sharma's conclusion to himself. "*Well, that's great. Sure cleared up the mystery for me too,*" Tommy was telling himself sarcastically, not caring who "heard" his thoughts. Commander Thren saw Tommy looking wide-eyed around the chamber trying to make some sense of where he was and mostly with whom he was. The Commander anticipated Tommy's question and "spoke" first, "*Tommy, I know that after all that has been happening to you, this is going to be difficult to understand. Very simply, we're what you would call 'visitors' here. Here on your Earth.*"

"Uh, you mean that you're from outer space?" Tommy said aloud, his eyes wide in surprise. He didn't bother to think-speak. How else could he put it? What do you say to an alien? It's not like you meet one every day.

"*Outer space? Is that what you call it? Well, I suppose that's as good a description as any. We are from the planet Carisor, of the Saltar galaxy. We are visiting here on a special science mission to research the environments of several planets in solar systems which support advanced life forms. Specifically, we are looking at the impact of solar radiation in the ultraviolet spectrum on life forms when the natural barriers to that light deteriorate or disappear. Do you understand, Tommy?"*

The Commander was "speaking" to him as an adult. Not like his teachers or even his parents. He looked directly at the Commander and without uttering a word but nodding said, *"Yes, sir, I think so."* Although, it was impossible to tell, he almost thought that Commander Thren had changed that pucker to a smile. Tommy was pleased with himself that he could communicate with these aliens. He didn't know how he did it, but however it happened, it worked.

Commander Thren looked at Tommy, *"Thank you, and welcome, Tommy Flagg. I must leave you for a time, but Arnul will see that you are comfortable."* The Commander nodded to Arnul; he then turned and walked back toward the black wall from where he had emerged moments earlier. Just as suddenly, the narrow red line shot up, scanned across, left to right, and Commander Thren disappeared into the blackness. Then the red line winked out.

Arnul turned to Sorgo and Glefon. *"I think that it would be best for Tommy to stay with the two of you in the crew quarters. Tommy, is that agreeable to you?"*

"Uh, sure, sir," Tommy said aloud, and then repeated the same in his mind - without the "uh".

"It's all right, Tommy, we can understand both sound wave and thought projected speec." the first officer said gently. He

added, "*As Sorgo and Glefon escorted you here, they will be your escorts for the remainder of your stay here. They will take you now to see Sharma and then to your quarters.*"

"Excuse me, First Officer Arnul..."

"*You may call me Arnul. Except for the Commander, we do not have such formalities here. What is your question, Tommy?*

But even before Tommy was able to frame the words in his mind, Arnul came very close to Tommy, put a bony four fingered hand ever so lightly on Tommy's shoulder and communicated, "*No, Tommy, Doctor Sharma is what your people call a male. I am female. Sorgo and Glefon are also females.*"

Tommy could only manage a weak, "Oh." He then started to think, "*But how can you tell the diff...*". He tried hard to stop thinking, but it was too late. Arnul "heard."

"*It's easy, but you need to be a Carisian to appreciate the difference. I must go, too. Please excuse me. Welcome once again, Tommy Flagg.*" Arnul bowed slightly and disappeared into the dense black wall the same way as Commander Thren.

Tommy turned to both Sorgo and Glefon trying desperately to keep his mind clear of any more thoughts about boys and girls, differences, clothes, names and titles, or anything else which would give him away to another embarrassing thought.

Sorgo sent a thought to Tommy, "*Please follow me, Tommy.*" She turned around and led Tommy toward the blackness on the opposite end of the chamber as Glefon brought up the rear.

Tommy looked straight ahead trying to focus on something that would tell him where the wall began in the darkness, and waited with growing apprehension for the red light which he realized opened a pathway of some kind. Tommy thought that he could sneak a quiet thought, *"Keep your mind clear; don't think about anything and don't look down at her backside...ahh, blast, I did it again."*

"Yes, Tommy?" You were trying to communicate something?" Sorgo asked as she turned to look at Tommy.

"Uh, no...no, Sorgo, uh, it was nothing." Tommy said aloud. He closed his eyes, shook his head and blew a lungful of air. *"How do you keep a secret in this place?"* he asked himself and only himself.

"We have none," Glefon added for good measure.

"Oh, boy," Tommy muttered under his breath realizing that there was absolutely no place to hide here.

"Oh, boy?" Glefon repeated.

Tommy shook his head and slapped his forehead. "Just an expression, Glefon, just an expression," Tommy tried whispering.

It suddenly occurred to Tommy that although Sharma said he was not one of them, Sharma did not say anything about Tommy's face. In fact, no one had even noticed. *"I may not be one of them, but I kinda look a little like them, sort of. And none of them laughed at me or called me ugly. They may be from outer space, but they're OK. I think I like them."*

Tommy was shocked to be receiving two signals at the same time. It seemed that both Sorgo and Glefon heard him. *"Tommy, we're not ugly and you're not ugly; and we like you. Please explain like."*

For the first time since the accident, Tommy smiled. It hurt a little because the smile stretched the skin on his face. And then he started to laugh. "Like? Like? Well, it's just like. You know, when you like someone. Or when you love,... No, no forget that. Let's see, "like"...well, it's like this...."

"How do you explain 'like' to an alien? he tried to think to himself. And then he smiled...and laughed. Really laughed. An out loud laugh for the first time in so long, and it felt good.

They continued to march single file toward the black wall that now loomed up in front of them. Tommy's voice echoed merrily in the chamber even as a red line appeared from the floor just a few inches in front of him. In the blink of an eye, the line silently slid across the dark wall and Tommy stepped through.

CHAPTER 19

This was not a day for being outdoors; certainly not in a painstaking search of several hundred square miles of slushy terrain beaten relentlessly by a driving wind and cold rain. Scott's friends and neighbors had already been up at first light and were doing there best to brave the weather. But Scott could see that they were growing weary. They were also wet and damp right down to their socks. They were farmers and tractor operators, not trackers; just fair weather weekend hunters and campers, and then only in a four wheel Winnebago with a waiting beer or hot coffee.

There was no easy way to do this, Sheriff Kanter thought to himself. They had been out in the bush now for two days. This was the beginning of the third. Not in 25 years on the job had he seen anything quite like this. **Vanished.** It was the only word for it. The State Police had joined the search with helicopters and sophisticated heat imaging and motion detectors. Back at the State Police Crime Laboratory computers calculated waypoints and arcs of distance assuming a complete range of walking and running speeds based on Tommy's height and probable stride. They had tried everything. But wherever they forecasted Tommy's location based on the direction of his last recognizable tracks, Tommy wasn't there. And not even a trace. Nothing. Tommy had just vanished.

His tracks ended at the bottom of the same ravine where he had his accident two months earlier. They saw the spot where he had fallen, saw the blood stained rocks; and even saw his imprint in the mud...but then nothing. He was there one minute, and then he wasn't. Scott heard a tired member of the search party mutter something about "weird and supernatural forces".

The Sheriff was sitting on one of the large boulders near the spot where Tommy had fallen earlier. He was staring at the small depression in the ground evidently made by Tommy as he lay injured and battered from a fall into the ravine...a second time. Scott went over and sat beside him.

"Sheriff, have you heard what some of the men are saying?"

"Scott, don't pay them any mind. They're tired, hungry and wet. Next thing they'll be suggesting monsters and space ships," Sheriff Kanter said sarcastically.

"But we have no idea, Sheriff. We have nothing, " Scott said shaking his head as it bent down to his chest. He fought the urge to sound devastated but realized that he wasn't doing such a good job. He too was tired, cold and discouraged. "I don't know what else to do, Sheriff. I promised Joanna I would stay out here until I found him...." and taking a deep breath, he swallowed and struggled to finish the last of the sentence, "...however, it ends up." He had not wanted to think that way, especially for Joanna's sake, but he was feeling he had run out of time and luck. There were no more answers; just strange questions which were getting more mysterious as they lingered at the spot.

Even as the Sheriff watched the men on their hands and knees searching the same ground for the third day, he knew that there was nothing else that could be done. They had found Tommy's last location. They had been able to recreate his movements and determine how he got there. They knew that he had attempted a frontal assault on White Bluff by going up the shale slide; he then had worked his way over to the left edge of the precipice and because it was dark, he probably never knew how close he was all the time to the edge. They found his tracks going up, and then found the point where he must have slipped and tumbled headlong back down into the ravine. And, yes, the weird thing was, that it was almost at the very same spot where the bus had come to rest. They had all the pieces of the puzzle except the last: Tommy himself.

The Sheriff put his arm around Scott and said as softly as he could, "Scott, I think it's time, don't you?"

Scott jumped as if he had been struck in the back. His head whipped up and his face contorted with white rage at the Sheriff. He reached out and grabbed the front of the Sheriff's jacket and held it as if he were about to shake Sheriff Kanter. He wanted to scream, "NO! Tommy's my son and he's out here somewhere. No, you can't just give up!" But the words wouldn't come out. Scott just held on to the jacket and looked into Sheriff Kanter's eyes. They were sad and tired eyes; eyes that had seen this kind of tragedy before. The Sheriff said nothing, but he knew what was coming. Scott's hands were white as he clutched the Sheriff's jacket and his arms and back were shaking. His jaw was set and hard. His eyes seemed to bore through the Sheriff and focus on something somewhere else. Then the tears began to well in Scott's eyes and his whole body began shaking as if he were suffering from a convulsive fever. He shook but held fast to the Sheriff who never moved. Scott's mouth began to twist. His lips quivered. Softly, he uttered, "Tommy, where's my Tommy. Sheriff, where's my Tommy." The Sheriff reached his arms around Scott and pulled him closer. And Scott buried his head in Sheriff Kanter's jacket and cried. His body heaved with sobs. The others stopped their search and each slowly walked over to the Sheriff and Scott.

They crowded around, some whispering a reassuring word; others put an arm around Scott. "Hang in there, we'll find him...we'll find him. Whatever it takes, no matter how long."

The rain fell in torrents and the wind drowned out the voices. It was going to be a long, hard search.

Tommy where are you?

CHAPTER 20

As Tommy, Sorgo and Glefon stepped through the black passageway, Tommy looked over his shoulder and saw the thin red line travel from right to left. In the same instant that they passed from the Atmospheric Transition Chamber, the lights went on. Actually, they weren't lights at all, it was more of a glow. Everything, including his two companions was bathed in purple. Beyond them, everything melted into a dark purplish haze and beyond that complete darkness again.

Tommy turned his head to look at Glefon and thought, "*Now you've turned purple. You look weird.*" And as he smirked at Glefon, he ran into Sorgo who had then stopped. Tommy's hands instinctively went up to push himself off, and in so doing touched Sorgo's back and made a rather startling discovery. His hands had sunk into Sorgo's back, and felt as if they were going to come out through Sorgo's chest. Although the skin of the visitors looked smooth and supple like silk, it had the same feeling Tommy remembered as when his Mom let him punch down dough after it had risen. That's it. It felt squishy, like dough. Embarrassed, he withdrew his hands as if he had touched a hot plate, but he looked at his fingers just to make sure that their skin, like dough, didn't come off on his hands. "OOPS, sorry, Sorgo. I didn't mean to rush into you. I was just looking...

Sorgo seemed not to feel, or even to notice that Tommy had nearly put his hands through her, *"Tommy, we are in the Ionic Purifier. It removes from us any lingering traces of your atmosphere which we may have accidentally picked up from our visit to the Outside. Your air is extremely toxic to us. We will need to remain here for a few moments to complete the decontamination process."*

"What about me?" Tommy said worriedly out loud, but he noticed that his "bubble" was still surrounding him.

"That is right, Tommy. Your bubble keeps you in your atmosphere. The Purifier will not have any affect on your bubble." Sorgo projected his thought and that peculiar calming feeling to Tommy. Tommy felt reassured, but it did not prevent Tommy from feeling like a lone gold fish in a bowl and asking the question: "Sorgo, you mean that your air is cleaner than ours?"

This time it was Glefon who replied, *"The molecular composition of our Carisian atmosphere is different from yours, and yes, it is cleaner."*

Tommy did not quite understand this "molecular composition" stuff, but he wasn't too sure that he liked the idea of "hearing" that their air was cleaner than his. Glefon ignored Tommy's reaction and continued without any hint of emotion or expression, *"Your air is contaminated with substances which differ greatly from the air your bodies were designed to breathe."*

Tommy was getting annoyed with Glefon.

"Glefon, I don't understand. What are you saying. Speak English. Well, you know you what I mean. Speak normal, would you please?" He was about to say "like a normal human being", but that wouldn't apply, would it.

He hoped that Glefon had heard, or felt what he was feeling. Apparently, Sorgo did.

*"Tommy, Glefon is saying that your air here on Earth is not pure. And as a scientist, Glefon is telling you that the air you are breathing is very different from the air your bodies **should** be breathing,"* Sorgo conveyed her thoughts over to Tommy trying to be as understanding and gentle as she knew how to be with these strangely emotional creatures.

"Well, why couldn't she say that in the first place?" Tommy said as he shot a glare to Glefon who was oblivious to the custom of humans glowering at one another. Tommy continued to stare at Glefon and then added, "Do you mean air pollution?"

"Your air is toxic to you as well," again Glefon transmitted her thought with simple and complete frankness almost as clinically as Doctor Sharma had spoken. Tommy was at a complete loss for words and had a stunned look, a sign that Glefon took to mean to continue. And she did with another simple and even more profoundly shocking

revelation, no less shocking because it was transmitted wordlessly: *"Some day, your people too will need Ionic Purifiers."*

Just then the purple glow disappeared and the red light shot from the floor on the opposite end of the Ionic Purifier. Sorgo turned toward the scanning red line and without turning her head sent a thought to Tommy, *"Decontamination is completed. Please follow me, Tommy."*

Tommy stepped through the passageway that suddenly revealed a dim, almost gray light on the other side. He was now in what appeared to be a very long corridor, and there were walls he could see this time. In fact, the corridor appeared so long that the walls seemed to converge somewhere in the distance. The walls like the light were a gray metallic color and were broken up by passages leading off into other directions. These corridors too seemed to disappear off in the distance. But there were no doors, anywhere, or at least, no doors as he understood them.

As they moved along the corridors, Tommy encountered other visitors- he felt that calling them "Visitors" now was OK. "Aliens" or "creatures" were only for horror movies. They were all the same height, and with the same features, and, well, Tommy still couldn't see any differences whatsoever. *"I still don't know how they can tell each other apart,"* he tried to think to himself. He looked at both Glefon and Sorgo for a thought reaction. Neither of them had heard, or at least reacted to this puzzlement. As each Visitor passed the three of them, each turned to look at Tommy, and each sent a thought which glowed with a warmth that Tommy could feel all over his body, *"Hello, Tommy Flagg. Welcome."* By the time Tommy had passed his tenth visitor, he stopped returning his own greeting aloud: "Hi!" He realized that he was getting better at transmitting his thoughts. The next visitor got a silent but no less enthusiastic, *"Hi!"* Tommy could also feel the gentleness that flowed from these people. No, he was positive now that they weren't going to hurt him. But, he wasn't too pleased about another Thoron scan by Doctor Sharma, though. No one stared at him. Maybe, they saw a resemblance, sort of, like Sorgo and Glefon did. But by now, they probably all knew that he wasn't one of them, and that he didn't look like other Earth people, either. But it impressed Tommy that these people didn't care. They just accepted him and welcomed him. *"I like these people, I really do,"* he thought, hoping now that everyone had heard him.

They did. In fact, the entire Carisian crew at Station - 3PS-204 had heard.

Sorgo continued to lead the way with Glefon in the rear. Tommy noticed in this dim light that his friends, yes, now he could now consider them friends, had an unusual way of walking. Sorgo and Glefon moved effortlessly, as if they weren't walking at all, but gliding. Then Tommy observed that he really wasn't walking either. Well, his legs were moving as if he were walking, but it felt strange. He could still feel the pain in his leg because of the fall, and that alone should have prevented him from walking, but in fact, he was walking. Sort of.

Actually, he was gliding too. His feet felt as if he were skating or sliding on ice but without ice skates. Through his shoes he could almost feel the absolute smoothness of the floor. Strange. It reminded Tommy of the smooth and silky feel of Sorgo's skin.

Sorgo "heard", and so did Glefon. Glefon immediately provided the scientific response to Tommy's thought: *"Interstitial organic thellenium membranous fiber."* Fortunately for Tommy, Sorgo interjected: *"The floors and the walls here, Tommy, are made of a special material, a combination of fiber like your clothes and metal."* Sorgo thought to herself that wasn't quite true; but it would do for Tommy. She felt that she was learning how to communicate with him as an Earth person and at his level. Glefon, who was "listening" to Sorgo's infantile elementary physics lesson launched into a very didactic explanation to the contrary - something about a process of fusion of living tissue with the hardest metal in the universe - Thellenium - to produce a synthetic product of unequaled strength, durability and use. Glefon began, *"Actually, it is not a combination, but a sub-atomic fusion process producing...".*

Sorgo led them down one corridor after another, turning left or right. Glefon was transmitting a continuing stream of Carisian chemistry, engineering and other stuff which did nothing more than clutter Tommy's head, *"...which then binds the Thellenium molecular structure with cloned Carisian proteins.."* It seemed they had walked miles. All the corridors looked the same to Tommy. He did not see any signs, markings or direction arrows. No "Exit" signs here. Just windowless and doorless corridors bathed in a dull grey light which seemed to emanate from behind the ceiling. There weren't any light fixtures either.

Again, Sorgo stepped in to rescue Tommy from Glefon's well meaning but mind boggling lesson on the thermodynamic properties of Thellenium, "I *must interrupt, Glefon, we have arrived at Medical Officer Sharma's chamber.*"

CHAPTER 21

Scott and Joanna Flagg sat at the kitchen table, opposite one another; neither had spoken for quite some time. Joanna prodded and pushed her dinner from one side of the plate to another. Outside, the rain had changed to snow, bringing yet another Spring snow storm. They could hear the wind moaning through the chimney. Her mind wandered, and she thought of Christmas cards and the pretty way they pictured snow piling up at the corners of each window pane. She remembered walking down the path to their door and she could see Tommy through the front window as he was lying under the Christmas tree in the living room. He had pleaded with her to allow him to study under the lights of the tree. "Don't worry, Mom, I promise I won't ...."

"I'm sorry, Joanna. I'm sorry." She heard Scott say and it made her scowl as it broke her waking dream about her baby, her Tommy.

She could hear herself, wooden and stiff. She wasn't angry with Scott and the others. They had tried. She knew that they had tried their best. "It's all right, Scott. I know," is all that she could manage to say to her husband. She was so tired. This was all a bad dream...all of it. The accident, the hospital, Tommy's disappearance. Tomorrow she would wake up and everything would be just like it was...

CHAPTER 22

Tommy couldn't understand it. There was no door, no sign; no indication whatsoever that they were at Doctor Sharma's office. All he could see were blank gray walls. And then in the blink of his eye, just as before, the bright red line appeared at his left foot and shot up to a point about 12 inches above his head. *"No room in this place for six footers,"* he thought. No thought reaction. Tommy was almost tempted to reach out and touch the red light, but he thought better of it.

Immediately after the red line scanned across the wall, the three of them slipped in. Tommy looked around him. By comparison to the Atmospheric Transition Chamber and the Ionic Purifier, this was a small room, gray again, but at least, Tommy thought, it really did resemble a room. *"Gray again, everything in this place is gray. I have to ask Glefon, ...no, not Glefon. I'll ask Sorgo why everything is gray."* The next thing that struck him was that one entire wall was full of blinking lights and several screens flashing what looked like numbers, charts, and graphs. He saw a table on the right with bottles, beakers and jars on it. Doctor Sharma's desk, he supposed. Off to the left, he noticed a very large glass container. It looked to Tommy like a large drum; more like a tank, actually lying on its side except that this tank appeared to be suspended in mid-air. One end of the tank was open and had a slab of metal extending from the opening. It looked like a silvery, flat tongue sticking out. There were lots of blinking lights on it and around it. That piece of machinery looked serious as he gave a shiver. At the opposite wall was a table with a large cabinet behind it- that must be the examining table Tommy concluded.

He then noticed that there were several Carisian friends waiting to greet him, although for the life of him he still couldn't figure out who was who. One of them stepped forward and thought spoke, "*Hello, again, Tommy. I am Doctor Sharma...No, Tommy, there will be no need for another Thoron scan,*" the doctor said in response to Tommy's unspoken concern. "*Please lie down here,*" the doctor said gesturing to the examining table. It was identical to the ones he had seen when he lived Outside with his parents.

Almost immediately, he reacted to his thought using the word "Outside." He was still trying to figure why he was thinking that the world with his parents was now "Outside" when the doctor motioned to Sorgo and Glefon to assist Tommy on to the table. Tommy winced with pain. Although, the floor and the bubble had made getting around easier, he still felt the pain in his leg and his chest from when he fell earlier. When was that? It had seemed so long ago...ages, in fact, but the pain reminded him that it was all too recent. For an instant, he thought of the field, the forest, falling, his parents...

Doctor Sharma came around to the table, and gently putting his bony hand on Tommy's shoulder thought transferred, *"Tommy, the Thoron scan reveals that you have fractures in several bones in your chest. I believe you call them "ribs". Your leg has been severely bruised, but there are no fractures. The worst problem is the effect on your hands and feet from exposure to the severe cold. Are you in much pain, Tommy?"*

"Yes, I guess I am, Doctor Sharma. Now that we're here and not moving around like we did in the Chamber and the Purifier, I'm really starting to feel it," Tommy responded weakly. "Mostly, it's my chest. It hurts when I take a deep breath," Tommy said aloud. Tommy saw Doctor Sharma nod in understanding. It was too complicated to try to convey by thought. Besides, he was hurting; he was tired, hungry and only now beginning to realize and to feel what had happened to him. No, what *was* happening to him. Who could possibly believe this? Was it really happening to him? Thoughts and feelings were suddenly cascading into him and then overflowing like water spilling over a dam. Tears welled into his eyes. And as he lay there, they began to stream from his eyes down the side of his face and into his ears. Doctor Sharma's finger which resembled more a twisted and gnarled twig slowly and gently, ever so gently, touched the flow of tears, but then only for an instant. He brought his finger up to his round dark eyes and then tilted his head first to the left and then to the right, but his eyes never moved from the tip of his finger. There was absolute "silence" in the room.

"What does this signify, Tommy? Is it related to your pain?" the doctor projected.

Tommy couldn't bother to thought-speak. "It hurts, Doctor Sharma. It hurts so much now. I think I want to go to a real doctor; to Doctor Joe in the hospital. He'll know what to do," Tommy stammered between sniffling. He rubbed his tears away with the sleeve of his dirty jacket leaving a smudge of mud across his face.

Another Friend stepped forward. Commander Thren. *"Tommy, this is Commander Thren. As I said earlier, you may leave any time and we will arrange to take you Outside. I want you to know that we, Doctor Sharma, can also help you and will do so if you wish it."*

The pain in Tommy's chest was growing worse by the moment and his hands and feet were starting to throb too. He was past the point of objecting. He sure wished that his Mom were here and Doctor Joe too. They would know what to do. They would put it right.

But they weren't were they? And he couldn't last much longer with the pain. He knew that there was something very wrong inside of him; and he couldn't feel his toes and his feet either. He didn't have the strength or the desire to transfer his thoughts; so he said aloud, "OK, sir, OK. It just hurts so much now. I can't breathe very well. It's like my chest is on fire." Tommy screwed his face to brace himself against the growing pain.

Tommy didn't notice the nod Commander Thren gave to Doctor Sharma; and with his pain he didn't "hear" the Commander, *"You may proceed, Sharma."*

Doctor Sharma walked back to the examining table and transferred a thought to Tommy which, if it had been spoken aloud, would have sounded like a gentle whisper. And with that whisper, the doctor also sent a warm projection. *"Tommy, in a moment, you will go to sleep and when you awaken, I think that you will feel much better. Are you ready?"*

Suddenly, Tommy was terrified. Alone somewhere, who knows where, with aliens with weird mouths and squishy skin. "I think I want to go. I have to go home to my Mom and Dad. I have to get up," Tommy said hysterically. Doctor Sharma stepped back to allow Tommy to sit up. Tommy tried to pull himself up, but the sudden stabbing pain in his chest made him cry out in pain and fall back on to the table. Overcome by fear and desperation, Tommy turned his head from side to side and called out, "Where am I? What am I doing here? Who are you people? Please help me. Somebody please help me. I want to go home."

Despite the haze in his mind from the pain, Tommy realized where he was; and that these people were his friends. They had rescued him from dying in the ravine, hadn't they? They made him feel welcome, hadn't they? And, most of all, they had accepted him for what he was...and no one had called him "snake face", had they? "It's going to be all right," Tommy thought to himself. "These are my friends." He then reached both arms out from his side and with the palms of his hands upward, called softly, "Sorgo? Glefon?"

Sorgo and Glefon stepped forward. Sorgo took Tommy's left hand with her little bony hand; Glefon took the right hand. Tommy turned to his left, and looked deeply into her dark eyes and calmly thought, "Sorgo?...It is you, isn't it?" Through the pain, somehow Tommy knew and forced a small smile. "*Yes, Tommy, I am Sorgo. Don't worry, all will be well. I have been treated here as well.*"

Glefon quickly added a thought, "*The musculoskeletal connective tissue regeneration procedure is really quite painless, Tommy.*"

Although is wasn't necessary between Carisians, Sorgo shifted his eyes from Tommy to look at Glefon and communicated what had to be the closest thing Tommy had heard to a reprimand, "*Glefon, could you offer something a little less clinical?*"

Silence. No thoughts passing. Glefon looked at Sorgo, then to Tommy and after a brief moment "spoke": "*Tommy, once I required a percutaneous skeletal fixation of a calcaneal and talus fracture which...*"

Sorgo hastily added: "*She broke her left foot...*" Tommy started to laugh, but it hurt too much to go on laughing. Glefon continued as if she had not heard Sorgo's clarification: "*...requiring the same procedure you are going to have.*"

Surprisingly, Tommy looked at Glefon and asked hesitantly, mostly for fear of the answer, "Did it hurt?"

"*No, Tommy, not at all,*" Glefon responded simply, and gently

Tommy turned to the left and then to the right and asked, this time in his thoughts, "*Sorgo, Glefon, will you both stay with me?*"

After looking over to Sharma who nodded his assent, both of them responded, "*Yes, Tommy, we will.*" With a firm grip on their bony hands, Tommy looked at Doctor Sharma, and took several deep swallows before he spoke, "OK, Doctor Sharma, ...I think I'm ready."

Sharma stepped around Glefon and came up close to Tommy's head. He reached behind the examining table and pressed several keys on a pad which opened the door to a cabinet. The doctor reached in and took out a crystal which resembled a very large M&M candy, about three inches in diameter. Like the Thoron scanner, it too glowed; but this one with a soft golden hue, like the setting sun on a summer's evening. Sharma sent both his thought and that warming feeling which brought a deep sigh from Tommy as he felt the reassurance it meant to give, "*Tommy, I am going to place this Protean Disc at the side of your head. In a matter of moments, you will feel a warmth come over you, and you will see waves of all the warm colors of light in your mind, and then you will fall asleep. And when you awaken, the procedure will be completed.*" Tommy was about to ask for how long he would be asleep, but without waiting for a question or a response, Sharma gently placed the glowing disc to Tommy's temple. Instantly, Tommy felt a warmth settle over him. It was like late Spring, not too cold, not too hot. He could almost smell the flowers on the Lilac bush under his window. It felt like T-shirt weather, but not sweaty. He looked over to Sorgo and Glefon. They were both still there, each holding one of his hands. The pain was there too, but something was happening...

As he tried to open his mouth to say something to them, he began to see a sparkle of light, well, a twinkle of gold, actually. The kind that you see when you switch on your Christmas tree for the first time on a wintry evening. The light slowly grew larger and larger. It didn't frighten him. He was awake, almost, but it felt like he was standing in a dream. He let the golden light wash over him, and he remembered the same feeling when he went to visit his grandmother at the seashore. Then another light immediately formed. This one was more orange. And it too grew larger as it approached him. He could feel himself relaxing; waiting for this orange wave to reach him. And then it did. It was a beautiful wave; soft and smooth, like Carisian skin. It enveloped him. And then he saw another wave, in the distance. This one was more yellow..."I think I'll wait for that one." And then there was another wave beyond that ...and one beyond that. Yellow, orange, gold....wave after wave...."Mom, you should see this. It's really neat."

CHAPTER 23

From a sound sleep, Joanna sat bolt upright in bed as if jolted by an electric shock. "Tommy? Tommy...is that you? I'm here. Where are you?"

Joanna's eyes tried to pierce the dark room expecting to reach out and see Tommy emerge from just beyond the darkness. She knew he was there. She could feel him, hear him, "Mom, it's really neat." That's what he said. She called out again, "Tommy?"

Scott woke after his wife's call to their son. "Joanna, you were dreaming. Tommy's not here. It must have been in your dream."

"No, Scott," she insisted, "It was no dream. I heard him. I know it. He's alive, Scott, he's alive! He's hurt. My baby's hurt, but...there's something else. I can't...I don't know what it is, but I don't think he's in danger...It felt strange. Almost like..." She hesitated, trying to find the words, then muttered so that only she could hear, "warm".

CHAPTER 24

Doctor Sharma looked down at Tommy. The glow of the Protean Disc had faded and then winked out. It had been programmed to emit only so much Protean radiation necessary to render the patient to a very deep state of sleep. Tommy was breathing slowly, but regularly. Except for the scars and welts, the pain, which had a few moments earlier twisted Tommy's face, had now disappeared. Tommy was blissfully asleep.

The doctor then directed Sorgo and Glefon to move the examining table with Tommy to the other side of the room, to what Tommy thought looked like the large barrel lying on its side. The barrel was in fact a Mass Accelerator Coupler, a high-energy spectromass synthesizer that would repair and regenerate the injured tissues in Tommy's body.

As Sorgo and his science partner, Glefon, gently transferred Tommy from the examining table to the table at the mouth of the Accelerator, Sharma conveyed, *"Glefon, initiate data transfer from the Thoron scan results to download into the Mass Accelerator Coupler. That will ensure that we have programmed the Coupler with all biomass details of Tommy's human body."* Other Carisian members of the medical group removed Tommy's clothes in order to attach various sensors that would monitor and record the restoration process.

When they had disrobed Tommy down to his underpants, the Carisians suddenly stopped and one sent a thought, "*Sharma, please observe.*" The doctor approached the medical team and saw that they were sending confused thought signals back and forth to each trying to decipher Tommy's Flintstones boxer shorts. "*Sharma, what is the significance of 'Yabba dabba do'?*"

"*Have you run the words through the data banks?*" Sharma quickly enquired.

"*Yes, Sharma, through all current Earth science and word lists from all Earth languages. We attempted past and current speech analysis and voice synthesizers. However, the words taken individually or as an expression do not appear to form intelligent and coherent thought or speech,*" one of the Carisians thought over to Sharma.

"*I do not think it relates to any part of Tommy's body, or represent any instruction as to its use. You may proceed,*" Sharma ordered. But he was not entirely pleased that they did not understand the meaning of these strange words, particularly before activating the Mass Accelerator Coupler. Almost as an afterthought, Sharma added, "*Keep checking those words.*"

After several moments of intense activity between the members of the team as Sharma and Commander Thren watched silently and waited, Glefon who had not left Tommy's side conveyed to Sharma, "*All data transferred; sensors and scans on line; Mass Accelerator Coupler indicates data accept; and shows all systems compatible with Tommy's. All of Tommy's body functions register within normal range for humans. Activation on your command.*"

Sharma transferred only, "*Activate.*"

With that, the slab extending from the Accelerator slowly withdrew taking Tommy inside the tank-shaped machine and then silently sealed itself. In the same instant the seal was completed, the entire wall behind the large device lit up with hundreds of blinking and twinkling colored lights. Tommy would have been reminded of the "Twinky Lights" which decorated the outside of his house during Christmas.

The Mass Accelerator Coupler stood there silent and ominous. From the viewing port on the side of this unusual "barrel", Sharma could see the darkness of the chamber within interrupted by repeating flashes of the brightest white light. He could see Tommy's face, peacefully asleep, now pale white, appear and disappear between each flash. "*Systems, please?*" he asked of no one in particular.

"*Power: At pre-set maximum; Ranges: Acceptable; Patient response: Normal,*" came the reply from one of the Carisians at the monitors.

"*Very well, advise me every tac* (* Carisian unit of time equal to 1 hour) *of system and patient status,*" Sharma ordered. He then turned to Commander Thren who had been standing close to the entrance of the medical facility "silently" observing and waiting for Sharma's report. As the monitors and lights glowed, and white flashes leaped out of the portlight from the Mass Accelerator Coupler into the grey lit room, everyone went silent as Sharma made his report to the Commander:

"Commander, Tommy is a young human; a male of that species; approximately three pel in age, between 10 and 15 years in human time. He had sustained serious injuries to his chest and leg in a fall, although these were not life threatening when we discovered him near the entrance to the Station. However, I do think had Sorgo and Glefon not returned him here, he would have expired from exposure to the cold. His resemblance to Carisians can be explained by severe trauma resulting in permanent damage to his facial and neck tissues from burns caused by a simple and very primitive combustion process which evidently produced a fire, although I cannot be certain of the events which brought on the fire."

"Why," Commander Thren asked.

"For the reason that we are unable to probe Tommy's mind on this subject. He seems to have erected very strong barriers even to our penetration. Amazingly strong, in fact - even for Earth people. It would appear then that his trauma extends not only to his body, but also to his mind."

Sharma waited for a "reaction" to his last thought statement. *"Please continue, Sharma,"* was all that the Commander conveyed.

"The combustion has grossly disfigured Tommy's face. There is no similarity now to his features before the trauma. The damage is irreparable; it is beyond the current technology of earth doctors to restore him. He repeatedly refers to himself in his thoughts as "snake face"; an apparent term of derision and ridicule from other humans of his age. I think that we can conclude he was suffering from abuse from these humans. The discovery of Tommy alone in this remote area at the time of day and at temperatures beyond human endurance, without food, shelter or adequate clothing is consistent with our theory that he was fleeing from other humans. That is all, Commander."

After "hearing" the report, Sorgo and Glefon came to the same thought, and the Commander "heard" it as if it were said aloud. So did everyone else in the room, including Commander Thren and Sharma. But, only the Commander would have asked the question: *"Sharma, can we repair his trauma?"*

Carisians did not have to look at one another when communicating. This time, however, the eyes of all the Carisians turned to Sharma. The operators at the Coupler monitor turned to look at Doctor Sharma. The doctor did not respond immediately. He was one of the most brilliant scientists in the history of the people of Carisor. They knew if it were within the realm of possibility, Sharma could and would find a way. After several agonizing moments, when only glances were shared in the room, Sharma turned his head and looked directly at the Commander, *"The answer to your question, Commander is binary – both yes and no."*

"Clarification, please, Sharma," Commander Thren conveyed. All eyes shifted back to Sharma.

"I believe we can repair his features, but we cannot repair the damage done to his mind," Sharma replied tersely. *"And there is another issue which I must bring to your attention with respect, Commander."*

"Proceed, Sharma," the Commander replied by thought transfer but already knowing what Doctor Sharma would say.

"It was the Council of the All Wise directive to all Carisor science stations that in no event were we to intervene in any matter of our host planets, regardless of the nature and severity of the consequences to our hosts. Our presence here must never be compromised. I must also point out, Commander, that we are already in violation. Repair of Tommy's internal injuries resulting from the fall and the cold would go unnoticed as no one apparently knows of these injuries and because the crude level of equipment used by Earth doctors prevents detection of anything we do here. Therefore, this intervention would probably go unobserved by the Earth people. But if we were to restore his face to its original state, there could be no explanation that we could program into this young human by Autosuggestion Implant to explain this dramatic change. Their equipment would disclose artificial skin and other repairs that are beyond their current technology. It would be irrefutable evidence that he was the subject of a very highly advanced medical

procedure unknown on this planet at this time in their evolution. It would most certainly intensify not reduce their search for some other explanation one of which will most certainly be extraterrestrial, or "Aliens" as Tommy has called us.

"*Thank you, Sharma,*" was all that Commander Thren responded. He then added, *How long will Tommy remain in the Mass Accelerator Coupler?*"

"*Cell regeneration in other lower life forms on this planet take about 4 tacs. I would expect that human cells, as they are more complex, would take longer. I have estimated approximately 8 tacs,*" the doctor replied to the Commander's question.

"*Please advise me when the restoration is completed,*" Commander Thren ordered. He turned and left the room.

For several minutes there were no thoughts conveyed by anyone in the room. Each Carisian was completely focused on one of the monitors. Only Sorgo and Glefon remained, looking at one another, not conveying any thoughts.

Doctor Sharma interrupted the "silence". "*Glefon, Sorgo. I expect Tommy will be hungry after the procedure. Intravenous Carisian feedings will be unsatisfactory and probably unpleasant for him. Please research a solution.*"

Glefon was the first to speak. "*I believe we already know, Sharma.*"

Surprise was not a Carisian emotion, but the doctor's quick response was as close to that emotion as possible. *"You do?"* he asked.

"When we came upon Tommy in the forest, we found this lying near him. It must have fallen out of his jacket cover. We saw him put some of the contents in his mouth from time to time," Sorgo explained.

"What is it?" Sharma asked reaching for the box from Glefon.

"Chocomonsters."

CHAPTER 25

"Joanna? This is Sheriff Kanter."

Joanna Flagg caught her breath for an instant as she heard the sheriff on the other end of the line. Why would he be calling she thought? She could feel her heart beat faster and her cheeks flush. "Yes, Sheriff?" she said hesitatingly.

"Joanna, I think you had better come down to the station. We might have something about Tommy." He didn't mean it to sound as ominous as it came out, but there wasn't any easy way to broach the subject of Tommy with his mother. Everyone knew that Joanna had been devastated by Tommy's disappearance. How long had it been now? Five, maybe six days? So much had happened. She knew that no one could have survived the frigid cold; followed by freezing rain; followed yesterday by another major snow storm. The mere mention of Tommy's name would start her shaking and crying. Still, there was news, albeit strange news. Probably nothing, but he had to tell Tommy's parents, strange and painful as it was. But it was painful for everyone, he thought. Everyone in the community felt as if they had lost their own child.

"He isn't....?" Joanna said in a husky, choked voice but then caught herself. She couldn't bring herself to think of Tommy gone... forever. No,... no, she was convinced that Tommy was alive, especially after that strange dream she had the other night. Bright lights; ...that warm feeling. No, Tommy wasn't...He was alive, somewhere out there...She shook her head, cleared her throat and started again, this time more positively, "What have you got, Sheriff?"

"Well, Joanna, it may be nothing, but we had a report from a trucker who was driving on the White Bluff Road the night that Tommy disappeared, and ...well,...I think you ought to come down here. Can you and Scott come right over?"

"I, I guess so, ...yes. I'll just call Scott and we'll be there in about an hour," Joanna said.

Joanna and Scott arrived at the Sheriff's office to be greeted by stares from the sheriff's deputies and the staff as they walked along the corridor. There was something strange about the way people were looking at her and Scott. Joanna thought to herself, it can't be surprise or grief. The Sheriff didn't say that Tommy was dead. These people all knew about Tommy. Some had even gone out on the search. But this was something different. Joanna could feel it. She looked at Scott who had felt it is as well. His eyes darted from person to person through squinted eyes as if looking for someone or something. It was a habit he had when he was trying to think something

through. "What is it with these people. What's wrong?"
he blurted aloud for everyone to hear.

They rounded the corner and met the sheriff standing at the entrance to his office. Scott was clearly agitated about the atmosphere he had encountered during the brief walk down the corridor. He said jerking his head back over his shoulder, "Sheriff, what's going on here? Have they seen a ghost or something?"

"Scott," the Sheriff said shaking his head and gently leading them into his office, "Scott, the word got out. You can't keep secrets in this town, or even in this office for that matter." He shut the door behind him.

"What word?" Joanna asked with a growing frown.

The Sheriff motioned for them to sit down. He was exhausted and wanted nothing more right now than just to sit. Besides, what he had to say to the Flagg's would be better if they were all sitting down. Scott and Joanna sat in front of Sheriff Kanter's desk, their eyes riveted on him, waiting, waiting for whatever it was that seemed to have everyone acting weirdly. The seconds seemed like an eternity.

Despite his fatigue, the sheriff suddenly looked almost pained. This was going to be difficult; very difficult indeed. He took a deep breath, and exhaled the words, "Well, it's like this..."

The Sheriff began his report slowly and very deliberately, "On the same morning, just as your telephone call came in reporting Tommy missing, I was reading the previous night's Incident Report from the deputy who had been on night duty. After your call, I dropped the report and came out to your place. In the next several days, with the search, and all the other activity, not to mention all the people rushing around this office coordinating the search for Tommy, I hadn't had the time to finish reading that particular Incident Report. Well, yesterday night was the first night I had time to catch up on my reading and something caught my eye.

"It seems that the deputy had received a call from a trucker who was using the White Bluff Road as a short cut to get to Ellenville. The driver had stopped his truck to check his brakes before heading down the steep road that crossed over the ravine where Tommy had his accident. When he got out of the truck, he said he saw several 'dots' of light, three actually, at the bottom of the ravine, near the spot where the bus had come to rest when it went down. At first, the driver didn't think anything of it. Hunters, probably, at a campfire; or maybe flashlights. But then he saw these three spots of light move. It couldn't be a campfire. It had to be flashlights. But if they were flashlights, the movements would be erratic, and jerky as the hunters climbed over the many rocks down there. But the lights weren't jerking; they were moving smoothly. ..No, not just moving; ... and here's where it gets strange...they were 'gliding' - those were the driver's exact words – 'gliding' in what seemed to be a formation. He had never seen anything like it before. First, I thought, helicopters, maybe? No, it was too low; well, below the tree line and there were no sounds of a chopper. Couldn't be a snowmobile either. There isn't a trail down there.

"The truck driver watched the lights 'glide' effortlessly over the rocky terrain, across the stream, and through the forest. He never took his eyes off them. Suddenly, the lights winked out. The driver kept looking at the spot where the lights went out, waiting for them to come back on again. After all, it was four in the morning. But the lights didn't re-appear. After about 15 minutes, the driver left. As he was driving, it occurred to him that maybe whoever was down there had fallen, so when he arrived in Ellenville, he called the deputy sheriff on duty and told him what he had seen."

The sheriff concluded his report, "I spoke to the trucker myself. He said he couldn't make out anything that looked like people. All he could see at that distance were the lights. I called the shipping company and had the trucker checked out. There's nothing to indicate that he would be making this up. I've asked him to come by the office so we can question him further. He's on his way." The he added, "That's it".

The Sheriff looked intently at his two guests. Waiting.

Silence.

Joanna sat there with her hands folded with the tips of her fingers at her lips as if in a prayer. She saw that Scott had that hard squinting look on his face. His eyes searched the sheriff's face. Joanna was about to speak, but Scott spoke first. His voice was cold and he had a glare in his eyes as he spoke each word, slowly and very deliberately, "That's not all there is to it Sheriff Kanter, isn't that right?" Joanna looked over at Scott and then at Sheriff Kanter. She didn't understand what Scott was ....

Before he answered, the sheriff sighed deeply. Yes, there was more, much more. **This** was the hard part. "Yea, there's more...I'm sorry, folks; I don't know how to tell you this. But, it looks as if he's been taken."

"What?" Joanna burst out. "Taken? Sheriff. What do you mean...taken?"

"It looks to me like he may have been kidnapped," the sheriff said gravely.

Scott started to shake his head and said, "But sheriff, how can that be? We searched every inch of that area for almost three days. There was no sign of a campfire; no footprints, human or animal; no sign of a struggle. Nothing. You said it yourself. It was as if he just disappeared. No, sheriff, I don't buy it. Maybe, the trucker did see lights moving, gliding; whatever. But hunters at this time of year? In this weather? It's not even hunting season." Scott 's voice started to rise. This was insane he thought to himself. Gliding lights floating at the base of the ravine, hunters in the off-season. Scott got up and said once again. "No, Sheriff, I don't buy it."

"I'm sorry, Scott. I haven't got anything else. I can't explain those lights either." And then he added, but regretted it immediately as he said it, "Have you got a better idea?" He was tired. Everyone was on edge. A ten-year-old boy was missing; and he didn't even have a single clue. Nothing. No footprints, no blood, ashes from a fire, clothing. Absolutely nothing.

Scott glared at the Sheriff and said coldly, "No, I don't Sheriff. You're supposed to be the expert."

The Sheriff flinched with the harsh remark. Joanna looked over to Scott and gave him a disapproving look and said, "Scott, the Sheriff's doing his best. Please."

Scott's shoulders sagged, more from frustration and fatigue than from defeat of any kind. "I'm sorry, Sheriff. I just don't understand. And, I guess I'm just worn out."

"It's all right, Scott. I understand. We're all tired. And this doesn't help," the sheriff responded softly. "But it sure does seem strange that on the night the trucker sees those lights, Tommy disappears in that ravine without a trace."

"Kidnapped," Scott struggled to say the word and then shook his head again. "I don't know. I just don't know."

The room fell silent again. Joanna broke the silence, "Sheriff, maybe he was kidnapped. But I know that whoever took him and wherever he is, he's all right. I know it."

The Sheriff conveyed a sympathetic look as she sat there slumped in the chair. But he saw something else: She really did mean it. No, she wasn't crazy, or a hysterical grieving mother. "He's out there. I know it, Sheriff. I just know it."

CHAPTER 26

"*Commander Thren, this is Sharma.*"

"*Yes, Sharma. Proceed.*"

"*As you requested, I am calling to advise you that Tommy is out of the Mass Accelerator Coupler.*"

"*His condition, please.*"

"*Restoration to his system is complete and successful. Tissue regeneration has resolved the injuries to his chest and leg. Damage to his hands and feet from exposure have also been corrected. His status is normal. All his bodily functions are normal. Upon regaining consciousness, he complained of hunger. Apparently, Sorgo and Glefon have resolved that.*"

"*How?*"

"*With a curious substance which we are analyzing for duplication. His Altara Wave Thought Projections have been monitored and indicate a high degree of pleasure during the consumption of this material which he has designated as ...Chocomonsters.*"

"*Very well, Sharma. Is there anything else?*"

"*He needs a considerable amount of rest and nourishment. I should think that after another twenty four tacs, he should be ready to return to the Outside. I have had him moved to the crew quarters with Sorgo and Glefon"*

"Thank you, Sharma, please advise me at the end of the 24 tac. We will meet in the crews quarters. I wish to discuss the trauma to Tommy's face..". Sorgo and other members in the crew quarters "heard" this conversation. Although it wasn't necessary, they looked at one another, then at Tommy who had not heard because he was literally stuffing Chocomonsters into his face and mumbling something like... "Where did Carisians get Chocomonsters?...You couldn't just walk in a supermarket."

One of the Carisian technicians finally broke the "silence". *"Tommy, what does Yabba Dabba Do mean?"*

Tommy laughed and as he did so spit out several of the brown nuggets and sent them flying across the room. The Carisians watched, monitoring his Altara Thought Projections...Amazing! Tommy felt great. The pain from the fall was gone. He wiggled his toes; and it didn't hurt to breathe. Tommy didn't know how they did it, but he was grateful.

CHAPTER 27

"Well, can you point out the spot where you saw the three lights?" the Sheriff asked irritably to Frank Gaines, the trucker who had seen the lights in the ravine. The Sheriff was exhausted and in a foul mood. After two weeks of tracking all over the ravine, talking to experts, and even consulting with a person who said she was a medium and was in touch with Tommy's spirit, he still didn't have a single clue as to Tommy's disappearance. He was no closer than the night Tommy was kidnapped. Yes, kidnapped. Tommy's parents were angry and upset about his kidnap theory; but some of the town's people were starting to talk about seeing strangers in town and posting guards at the roads leading to the town. He had even seen a few people carrying guns.

"Well, I can't be sure of the exact spot, Sheriff. It was pitch black, you know." The trucker sounded apologetic, and a little defensive as he saw the dark scowl on the Sheriff's face.

Trucker Gaines continued as he gestured, "This is about where I parked my rig. And I first saw the lights over there...just to the right of the bridge. They were moving in a zigzag pattern always to the right until they got to about over there when the lights went out." The trucker pointed into that same darkness while one of the

Sheriff's deputies swung an enormous light beam into the ravine following the trucker's finger. The light was the kind that could be seen at fairs and light shows sending beams of light high up into the air. Tonight the brilliant shaft of light penetrated the deep and forbidding ravine. Giant distorted shadows rose out of the ravine and danced along the ravine wall as the light swept across the crevasse. And the yellow eyes of the animals of the night stared up from their labors into the harsh glare. Evergreens were momentarily painted with a greyish-silver streak and then disappeared again in the darkness.

"Are you absolutely sure, Frank? That's the spot, right?" Sheriff Kanter persisted.

"Near as I can reckon, Sheriff. That's the spot down there," came the trucker's response.

"OK, this is what we're going to do." The Sheriff was still holding to the theory that Tommy was taken. Yes, it was far-fetched; hunters in the ravine in winter and in a storm; no signs whatsoever; no tracks; no ransom demand. But still, there was something about this case that gave the sheriff the feeling that this was not just about a missing boy. There was more to this than met the eye, but he just couldn't put his finger on it. After thirty years in this business you just know. There **were** kidnappers. There were **"other persons"** involved with Tommy's disappearance. Putting it that way made it easier for Tommy's parents and everyone else to look at it. But in his mind, it was plain and simple: some one or some persons had kidnapped Tommy, and if Tommy's mother's intuition was anything to go by, Tommy was still alive and very near here.

The Sheriff carefully laid out his plan to the deputies and the other volunteers. Two people would take round the clock watches at three-hour intervals. One spotter would be on the side of the ravine at the same spot where Trucker Gaines stopped. The other spotter would take up his observation post on the other side of the ravine. They would be in continuous contact with each other and with the Sheriff's office by radio. The White Bluff Road was sealed off. If there was anyone in the ravine, they were trapped down there.

"Report anything suspicious before taking any action. We don't want to scare them into doing anything we'll regret. Got it?" the Sheriff said gravely at the town meeting where he announced his plan and put up the volunteer sign-up sheet. Privately, the Sheriff gave his plan two weeks. If the kidnappers, or whoever, were down in that ravine, they had to reprovision, or make some move which would give them away. After that? Well...we'll just have to take it as it comes, he concluded.

Scott Flagg thought this was the craziest thing he had ever heard. He was convinced that Tommy was gone, and maybe even dead, but not kidnapped. No, that was impossible. But whatever had happened to Tommy, his wife kept insisting that Tommy was still alive and warm and...well, she said, "happy". He wanted to say something like she was "in denial", and that no one could have survived the exposure for so long a time. He couldn't bring himself to burst her balloon. She would have to come to the realization herself: Tommy was gone. But for Joanna, he volunteered to take his watch assignment along with the other volunteers.

They sat in their cars or pick-ups facing one another on opposite sides of the bridge crossing the ravine. The hours dragged by, broken only by the occasional calls from the spotters in the observation post. It was more to break the monotony, and to keep each other awake than to report a sighting.

"See anything?" began a typical spotter's report to the other.

"Nope."

"Roger that," came an attempt at professionalism just to extend the dull conversation.

And so it went. The same - hour after hour. Then several days passed. Nothing. The dedicated radio in the Sheriff's office was quiet. And after three days, no one seemed to notice. The spotters, both deputies and volunteers, settled into the humdrum of a well worn routine, showing up at the assigned hour armed with jugs of coffee and donuts, struggling to stay awake during the early morning hour "graveyard shift", and then home to attempt to capture disrupted sleep.

But the boredom was about to be shattered. Actually, it was about to be shot...literally.

Deputy Sheriff June Killian was sitting in her patrol car listening to an all night talk show, and the constant chatter of other deputies on the police network, when it started.

"June, June, it's Steve, I think I see...yes...the lights, I see the lights! June get over here!" Steve Barker shouted frantically into the radio. "June, hurry, they're moving toward the bridge!"

June Killian sat bolt upright and as she did so spilled her coffee over her blouse, "Damn! Steve why are you yelling. Calm down. I'll take a ....OK, I see them. I'm coming over to you, Steve. Steve? Steve, where are you?"

As Deputy Killian pulled up along side Barker's pick-up, she could already see him disappearing into the night headlong down the ravine. She immediately flashed her seal beam lamp and found him running, and stumbling his way down the steep slope arms flailing to hold his balance. And she could hear Barker shouting, "Stop, stop...you down there, stop!"

"Oh, no," she groaned. She ripped the microphone off the radio. "Sheriff Kanter, this is June, do you read? Sheriff? Sheriff, come in." She sounded perturbed and the Sheriff knew it. "Go ahead, this is Kanter," he responded trying to sound calm, "What's the matter, June?" Deputy June Killian had been on the force for over ten years, and one of the best deputies he had on the force. She would make a good replacement when he retired. If she were upset, he knew her well enough to start worrying.

"Did you hear Steve?" she said recomposing herself as she held the mike in one hand, and scanning the ravine with the light in her other.

"No, I didn't, June. Go ahead," the Sheriff called back.

"Sheriff, it's Steve Barker. He's headed down the ravine. He saw lights, and..." She was about to explain when the Sheriff cut in. "Lights? He saw lights? June, did you see them? How many?" His voice was agitated and excited. This had to be it! He was right. They would come out. But, Steve Barker. He hadn't planned on that. Without waiting for her reply, "Can you still see him?"

"Hang on a minute, Sheriff. Yes, I can see still see him. He's stopped. Yes, I can see the lights; they're two lights. They've stopped moving as well. They must have seen or heard Barker. He's been shouting at them to stop 'in the name of the law' ".

Sheriff Kanter called back, "June, you've got to stop him. They may be dangerous. And I know he is dangerous. I'll be up there as soon as I can."

She had kept her light trained on Barker, but she could still see the two lights. They did seem to have "glided" just like the trucker said. They had stopped and hadn't moved for several moments. And then she realized. No, those lights weren't from any hand-held search light she had ever seen. No, those weren't lights at all. They were ...more of a glow in the dark...like the glow that fireflies make on an August night.

And then it happened. As she opened her mike to acknowledge the Sheriff's call, there was a "Pow!", a sharp sound that sent echoes bouncing off the walls of the ravine to fill the night. The Sheriff heard it in the mike.

Deputy Killian's eyes widened and her mouth gaped wide open. For an instant, she couldn't take a breath.

"June, what was that? June, are you alright?" The Sheriff almost sounded frantic.

The deputy resumed her quiet professional tone. "Sheriff, Barker has taken a shot. It looks like he may have hit one of them. One of the lights.... Hang on, now both lights are out."

* * *

He saw the glow first. Then he could see what was inside the glow. He was close enough to see...**them.** "Oh, what in the name of God... What is that, " he whispered in a ragged voice but not loud enough for them to hear. For several moments he was frozen.

The Carisians who must have read his thoughts turned to look directly at him, and Barker knew it. By God, he could feel it! They were looking at him! It almost felt as if they were talking to him. "*Mr. Barker, we mean you no harm,*" he thought he heard them say. Heard...heard, how could he hear anything, he thought. Yes, he had heard June Killian calling his name from the top of the ravine, but he was positive he had heard **them** too. It almost seemed that they were speaking directly to him.

"Oh, God, oh God! They're creatures...slimy, evil looking creatures," he croaked aloud. He knew he couldn't call June Killian. What could she do? She was at the top of the ravine. By the time she got down to where he was, well....anything could happen. "They

144

might take me too. Just like they took poor Tommy. Must have eaten him judging by the way they look."

Then he "heard" it again: *Please, Mr. Barker, do not be alarmed.*"

Alarmed? he thought, alarmed? I'm scared to death! No, this can't be happening! I hear them but I don't hear them. I see them, but their mouths aren't moving. And they look...evil. I have got to do something before they do something to me. I'm not going to end up like poor Tommy. No, sir.

He called out. "Who are you? Where's Tommy Flagg. Don't move or I'll shoot."

One of the Carisians lifted his arm in a Carisian gesture of peace.

Barker didn't see it that way.

He fired a shot.

The Carisian slumped over and at the same instant the protective bubble winked out. The other Carisian took hold of his comrade and instantly darted into the safety of the trees and back into the safety of the Earth Station.

"Jane, I got one! I got one! He tried to shoot me!" Barker screamed into the field phone.

CHAPTER 28

By this time Tommy had become quite familiar, almost comfortable in the crew quarters. For the first time in his life, he couldn't eat any more Chocomonsters. It seemed that these Carisians had an inexhaustible supply. Well, he wasn't going to complain. He wondered what would happen if he asked for hamburgers and French fries. Later, perhaps.

Tommy could see Sorgo hunched over one of the monitors, staring intently into the dark blue screen. Tommy approached from behind. He could see the screen only as a blur of scrolling symbols he had never seen before. Slowly, Sorgo turned sensing Tommy's puzzlement. *"It's a report, Tommy, on the information we have collected on the atmosphere on your planet. And I must say, it doesn't look very encouraging,"* Sorgo thought.

Tommy ignored Sorgo's "comment". It wasn't that he didn't care. There was still so much he didn't understand about his new found friends. Suddenly, he just wanted to know everything, all at once, and now.

Tommy couldn't bother to thought transmit his conversation. He was just too stuffed full of Chocomonsters even to try. "Sorgo, how come you know so much about us and how do you know our language, and where do you really come from, and where is your space ship...?" Tommy blurted out loud.

"Well, Tommy, it's really quite simple. On our way to Earth, we monitored your radio frequencies. We learned a great deal of your history, language and culture. Unlike Carisor, your Earth has many of each." She explained simply and gently.

It suddenly occurred to Tommy that the explanation was really quite simple and obvious. Of course. It made sense. But certainly not if Glefon had explained it. He mimicked the scientist, "We monitored your sub-light, low frequency, radio waves..." he thought remembering a science fiction movie he had seen.

Sorgo, of course heard, and conveyed, *"Well, done Tommy, actually, you are right on both counts: that is the technical explanation, and that is how Glefon would have explained it. And, as for the spaceship. There is none here now. We came many, many years ago; several thousand of your years in fact. Since then we have lived here underground in our science station designated 3PS-204. In fact, it is the largest of all our planetary research facilities.*

"By the way, Sorgo, where is Glefon?" Tommy asked aloud.

* * *

Seated in the Control Center, Commander Thren responded to a call from Sharma. *"Proceed, Sharma."*

"As you requested, Commander, it is 24 tac since I reported that Tommy is completely recovered. Do you wish to discuss his other physical problems?" Sharma transmitted.

147

Before he was able to complete his thought transmission, the Commander was suddenly interrupted by Arnul, the deputy commander of the Earth Station. Most unusual.

"Yes, Arnul, this is Thren. Proceed."

Arnul thought over to Commander, *"Commander, I wish to report a matter on the Torlant Network."* The thought sent a shiver throughout Earth Station 3PS-204. A communication on the Torlant Network? In an instant, the entire Earth Station was cross communicating furiously. It can't be. A Torlant communication? Here? Why? It was difficult for the Commander, let alone anyone else to think in the sudden jumble and clutter of communications buzzing in the air. Then just as quickly, the flurry of communications died down. Then silence, a long silence. Waiting. Waiting for the Commander's response.

A request to use the Torlant Network was a most extraordinary one. Carisians by nature had developed into a people who were completely open. There were no secrets; nothing to hide. The first lesson that every Carisian learned after reaching the First Stage was that openness was sacred; secrets were sinister. Anyone, anywhere could "listen" to any conversation at any time. However, the Council of the All Wise did recognize that there were rare times in the life of a Carisian when special circumstances existed which might require urgent, closed and secret communication. It was absolutely never used frivolously. To do so would incur certain condemnation and expulsion from the Planet Carisor. It had never been used during the mission of Earth Station 3PS-204. Arnul had never asked for a Torlant Network communication in her life.

The Commander hastily called to mind the Council directive on Torlant Network Communications:

> It is forbidden to communicate in secret between Carisians; except in the following coded circumstances: Code Alpha: the life of a Carisian is threatened by open communications. Code Beta: to report an imminent threat to all Carisians. Code Delta: an open communication would cause fear and disorder to Carisians.

It seemed an eternity was passing. There was absolute silence on the Earth Station. The Commander opened his mind. All he could sense was Tommy in the crew quarters enjoying his Chocomonsters, oblivious to the silence around him.

Slowly, almost painfully, the Commander responded, *"You understand, Arnul, the nature of your request?"*

"Yes, Commander, I understand," Arnul thought back to the Commander.

"Very well. Under which Code do you request the Torlant communication?" the Commander replied.

"Code Beta, Commander," came the succinct reply.

A long silence followed. It felt as if everyone on Earth Station 3PS-204 held his breath.

At long last the Commander responded, *"Torlant Network communication request granted under Code Beta. Proceed Arnul,"* the Commander thought ordered.

Immediately, all the Carisians turned off all internal communications monitors and transmitters on the Earth Station and stepped away from their consoles. In the Control Center, the Commander went to the nearest monitor and typed his access code to the Torlant Network. Arnul did the same from her work station in the Communications Center. At the same time, the Torlant Network was automatically opened and began transmitting the Codes to the Planet Carisor to the Council of the All Wise.

Arnul typed the following message that was simultaneously beamed to the Planet Carisor: COMMANDER, GLEFON HAS BEEN GRAVELY INJURED; AND I HAVE REASON TO BELIEVE THAT THE LOCATION OF EARTH STATION 3PS-204 HAS BEEN COMPROMISED.

The Commander typed his response: ACKNOWLEDGED. PROCEED. GLEFON FIRST.

GLEFON WAS STRUCK BY A HIGH POWERED PROJECTILE WHICH STRUCK HER IN THE CHEST AS SHE OFFERED THE CARISIAN SIGN OF PEACE. IT APPEARS THAT SHE HAS SUFFERED CONSIDERABLE INTERNAL INJURY. I FEAR

THAT SHE MIGHT NOT SURVIVE. I HAVE HAD HER MOVED TO THE MEDICAL FACILITY.

Arnul hesitated for a moment, then continued: OUR SENSORS HAVE DETECTED LOW ENERGY TRANSMISSIONS BOTH THERMAL AND INFRA-RED EMANATING FROM AIRBORNE CRAFT NEAR THE ENTRANCE TO OUR EARTH STATION. OUR COMMUNICATIONS MONITORS HAVE RECORDED TRANSMISSIONS TO THE EFFECT THAT THIS IS THE SPOT WHERE AN OBSERVER, IDENTIFIED AS A 'TRUCKER', SAW THREE WHITE LIGHTS GLIDING. THEY SUSPECT IT HAS SOMETHING TO DO WITH THE DISAPPEARANCE OF TOMMY. THEY INTEND TO PRESS THE SEARCH IN THIS AREA. COMMANDER, I BELIEVE SOMEONE, THE TRUCKER, SAW SORGO AND GLEFON ESCORTING TOMMY AT THE MOMENT THEY ENTERED THE EARTH STATION. Arnul waited for the Commander to take this news in, but she knew what the Commander would reply.

It didn't take long for the words to dance across the blue screen of Arnul's monitor: WHAT IS THE LIKELIHOOD THAT THEY WOULD DISCOVER THE ENTRANCE?

Arnul realized the impact that her following response would have on Carisor, the Commander and the crew of their Earth Station, 3PS204. She thought for a moment, then slowly typed: THE ENTRANCE IS HIDDEN BY

A PLASMA LIGHT SHIELD WHICH IS ACTIVATED ONLY BY THE SCIENCE TEAMS UPON LEAVING AND RETURNING. I BELIEVE THAT THE EARTH PEOPLE'S DETECTION EQUIPMENT ALTHOUGH VERY PRIMITIVE COULD DETECT THE EXTERIOR DIATRON ANTENNAE WHICH ACTIVATES THE PLASMA LIGHT SHIELD. IN SHORT, COMMANDER, YES, I THINK THEY COULD DISCOVER THE ENTRANCE TO EARTH STATION 3PS-204. THIS COMPLETES MY TORLANT NETWORK COMMUNICATION.

ACKNOWLEDGED, the Commander typed. After determining that Arnul had logged off her communication console, the Commander remained on the Network with the open line to the Planet Carisor. He waited, but he knew that for him the matter had only just begun. The cursor on the screen blinked rhythmically: 1,2,3,4...1,2,3,4...1,2...then the screen jumped to life.

COMMANDER THREN. ACKNOWLEDGE PLEASE, came the message dashing across the screen.

THREN, HERE.

COMMANDER THREN, THIS IS DORVEL.

YES, WISE ONE.

CHAPTER 29

"Sheriff, this is Chopper One, do you read?"

"Go ahead, Chopper One, I hear ya. What have you got?" Sheriff Kanter replied.

"Chopper One. Sheriff, it's strange, real strange. We're getting lots of interference on our high gain frequency channel. It's as if there were a NASA transmitter in the ravine," came the scratchy reply from the helicopter that hung motionless in the clear blue sky above.

Sheriff Kanter was leaning against the door of his car with the microphone in his hand and close to his lips looking up at the helicopter floating over the ravine. Scott Flagg was standing on the passenger side looking at the Sheriff. The sheriff spoke as if the pilot were standing in front of him. "Can you give me a fix, Mark, on the precise location of the interference?"

Mark Clauson. Actually, it was Colonel Mark Clauson, United States Air Force Special Tactical Squadron. He had heard the bizarre story of Tommy's disappearance and had volunteered his team to conduct a sweep of the area. The Colonel together with his team of electronics warfare specialists aboard the Bell Ranger were the best in the business and had the most sophisticated electronics gear at their disposal. If anyone could do it, these boys could, Sheriff Kanter thought. "Roger, sheriff, stand-by," came the business-like reply from the pilot.

The sheriff turned from his skyward glance to the deputy sheriff's car parked directly ahead of him. He called out, "Frank, are you ready?" Frank was Frank Gaines, the trucker who had stopped at this spot on the White Bluff Road and saw the white lights "gliding" across the bottom of the ravine.

"I guess so, Sheriff. I'll do my best. Remember, like I said the other day, it was dark when I saw the lights," came the trucker's reply.

Scott scowled and was about to say something, but the Sheriff called back, "Okay, okay, just do the best you can."

With that the trucker, accompanied by two deputies, two tracking dogs, their handlers, and several volunteers from the local fire rescue department began the painstaking trek to the bottom of the ravine. Overhead, the specially equipped helicopter began to fly crisis-cross patterns over the ravine. Scott began to drum his fingers on the hood of the car.

The sun was at its highest point in the Spring sky, but it didn't do much to warm the air. It was bitterly cold for this time of year. And the ground was still frozen. The Sheriff alternately watched the rescue team work their way further down the ravine and then skyward at the helicopter buzzing left, then right, then hovering. Scott noticed, however, that the area which the helicopter covered seemed to be getting narrower and narrower. Yes, they had found something, Scott thought. He knew it. Joanna was right - Tommy would be found any minute now hiding under a pile of rocks, and....

"Scott. Scott..."

Tearing himself away from the dream of finding Tommy, Scott had to shake his head and said, "Uh, sorry. Yes, Sheriff?"

"Scott, I think they've got a fix. Listen," the Sheriff said motioning to the helicopter as if he expected someone to shout from the craft.

"Chopper One, here. Sheriff?"

"Go, ahead. This is Sheriff Kanter."

"We have the coordinates of the point of maximum interference. That's the best we can do on the radio frequencies. I thought we'd cover all bases so we've also taken thermal images with our heat seeking photo equipment. We'll process it and have it over to you in a few hours. I'll drop her down as low as we can go in the ravine and drop a marker. We'll stand over the spot until your boys can converge."

"Roger, that, Mark. Standing by." The Sheriff then called to his deputies. "Lou, did you hear that?"

Deputy Louis White, sounding out of breath, huffed into the speaker of his field phone, "Uh,...yea...we ...a ..heard. We're almost there."

Slowly, the helicopter descended into the ravine careful of the treacherous winds which roiled up. Scott shielded his eyes as the craft descended in front of the sun. It settled lower and lower and then passed out sight. But they could hear the characteristic "Thick, thick thick" of the blades as they beat the cold air.

Now, all there was to do was wait. Wait. But for what? What would they find? Tommy? Somehow, that was not likely. Evidence of a kidnapping? Sheriff Kanter was beginning to think that Scott was right. They had gone over every inch of the ravine, including the area where the helicopter was descending. There were no signs of kidnap. And it was brutally cold for someone to be wandering around hunting. Scott too was thinking about that night when Tommy left. Tommy probably had heard him say some awful things to Joanna about Tommy. About his being ugly. God, forgive me, Scott thought. His heart was breaking as he thought about his son and his wife. Both men waited, each lost in his own thoughts. Hoping. Then...

"Sheriff, this is Lou, I think we have something. Just a minute..."

CHAPTER 30

For a millennium Carisians had been a people for whom logic, courtesy and restraint were the highest virtues. There was no room for emotions or emotional reactions from a right thinking Carisian. Anger, laughter, shouting, sadness and love were unheard of, certainly not in polite company anyway. Any Carisian who displayed any such emotions after having had the Hands of the All Wise placed on his or her head was certain to receive considerable re-education and programming on the peril of emotions and the risks it presented to good order on Carisor.

Commander Thren sat pensively for a long time in front of the now darkened screen. His Torlant Network Communication between himself and the Wise One had terminated. The decision had been taken. There was no debate, no argument, no shouting, and certainly no anger. The Council of the All Wise had decided. All that left was to obey, quickly and without second thought.

Earth Station 3PS-204 must terminate all activity, shut-down all but essential systems immediately and all personnel must make ready for departure. A Carisian craft in the Falarian galaxy would be notified to proceed to the Earth Station to rendezvous with the science team on Earth.

Thren had been in command of 3PS-204 for almost 2 pel. His team had learned much about the atmosphere of Earth. But it was the color of this planet with its brilliant blues, greens and browns that he would always see and hold in his mind to his last day. They were a vivid contrast to his dying home planet, once as beautiful, no, more beautiful than this Earth. Now, Carisor was shrouded in a thick grey fog. There was no day. No night. Just the suffocating gray. It blocked out the Carisian sun, the stars of the other galaxies and the planet's two moons, Casto and Jorn.

The scientists said simply that "the air had died". They studied and studied, but could find no solution. Once destroyed, there was no way to bring the planet back to life. Science teams such as his were sent out to the vast reaches of the universe to find a solution. Many were tried, but every attempt to bring Carisor back to life had failed.

For a long time now the people of the Planet Carisor had abandoned the surface and learned to live beneath the ground. It was a world of artificial light; processed food and water; synthetic fabrics; and building material. Everything natural had been consumed by the Gray Night above.

And as the Commander woke from his day dream, he felt...yes, felt. He felt sadness. A large sadness for his science team and his planet. As the entire station crew was still in Torlant mode, no one would attempt to "listen" to his thoughts. So, he held on to them for a very long moment. This was a very sad day.

But now it was time to act. *"All members, be advised that the Torlant Network Communication has terminated,"* the Commander communicated his thought to everyone. He then added very simply, but formally: *"All members of Earth Station 3PS-204. Please prepare for standard, non-emergency departure from this station. Arnul, you will execute emergency lock-out immediately."*

Without hesitation, Arnul who was already at the Communications station during the Torlant quickly went over to a special console, and entered her access code which immediately flashed a sequence of coded procedures. After completing the required briefing to the central computer, a small drawer opened near the console revealing a switch bathed in red flashing light. It was the detonator switch for the Diatron antennae which was positioned immediately at the access to the Earth Station and which controlled the Plasma Light Shield entrance.

Arnul flipped the switch. The entrance to Earth Station 3PS-204 was sealed forever.

CHAPTER 31

Deputy Sheriff Louis White bent over to reach for a small silvery wire like object that had caught the noon sun. The deputy would say later that it "looked like a twisted wire clothes hanger". But as he reached to pick it up, the silver suddenly grew brighter. It glowed first yellow, then red to purple, and then shriveled into a charred black mass. From the corner of his eye, he saw another "clothes hanger" about ten feet to his left turning the same color at the same time and burn to ashes as well.

"Sheriff, White here. There's something going on, and it ain't normal," the deputy reported into the field phone.

"Normal?" The Sheriff heard the word, but couldn't believe he had heard it. "What do you mean, 'it's not normal', Lou?"

"Sheriff, there was nuthin' here but two silvery wires spaced apart in front of the ravine wall. When I reached to look at one, well, they both just now burned down to black ash. I saw it with my own eyes.

There's nuthin' else here, Sheriff. No tracks, no cave entrance, nuthin' at all, but,...it's real strange, Sheriff. You know when you feel like you're being watched. Well, I get this strange feeling on the back of my neck...I think you better get down here. It's real weird."

Sheriff Kanter had known Lou White from when they were kids together. Lou was the best tracker in the state. None better. He knew the forests, and knew the animals. And if there was something down there that bothered Lou that much, that's all the Sheriff needed to convince him that there was foul play connected with Tommy's disappearance.

"I'm on my way, Lou," Sheriff Kanter called. In rapid fire, he began issuing order to his deputies. "Stan, call the State Police. Tell them I need a forensics team over here, fast. Better have bring along a small tactical unit as well. It could get hairy. Call Mark Clausen at the base. See if they have those thermograph photos ready. And I want this road sealed off. No one in or out." He then turned looking for his other deputy. "June, what have you got from Barker?"

"Not much, I'm afraid, Sheriff. He's in shock. Keeps going on about evil creatures, not human, no hair. And one tried to shoot him," June Killian replied.

"What do you think?" the Sheriff asked her. She too had good sense, maybe not of the forests like Lou White, but she had good instincts with people.

"I can tell you this. He's telling the truth about seeing people down there. And I don't think he's making up the fact that they were strange looking. Remember, he had an opportunity to look at them for some time before he felt threatened enough to shoot. But he's scared, Sheriff, real scared."

It was a few moments before she spoke. She had thought about not telling the Sheriff because it was so...wild, crazy, unreal. She watched the Sheriff's darkening face.

"There's more, Sheriff," she said gravely as she reached into her patrol car. "I think you had better take a look at this," as she handed him a crude drawing of a Carisian. "I asked him to tell me what the people in the ravine looked like and this is what he described." She had listened to him tell and retell the story several times now. He didn't change any elements of the story, including their descriptions, despite her very tough questions. She couldn't understand it either. What did he really see? And who or what is down there?

CHAPTER 32

Tommy was sitting comfortably with several Carisian technicians in the crew quarters oblivious of the growing storm of activity in the ravine. He was delivering an animated monologue about the evil Klingons in a Star Trek adventure, his favorite TV program. "Have you ever seen anything like them on your travels?" he enquired genuinely of his new friends.

Tosh, the eldest of the group sent a thought, *"No, Tommy, actually, we did not encounter intelligent life on our journey here."*

"Hmm," Tommy could accept that. "OK, then, let me tell you about some of the other things I do. Well, I go to school, but it's really boring, you know." Tommy hesitated and thought to himself, "Well, maybe they **don't** know."

They heard and Tosh responded. *"We know about school, Tommy, and young Carisians also describe school as tedious."*

"I love baseball. I'm the pitcher for my team. I'll bet you've never heard of baseball. And I love to play video games and eat hamburgers..." Tommy was getting better at transferring his thoughts. But, he also found that it was a very tiring

way to communicate. So, his conversations were a mix of words and thoughts. The Carisians, polite as always, listened to his every word, spoken or by thought transfer.

"...with fries and lots of ketchup," Tommy completed the sentence aloud. He was about to recite his entire albeit limited diet. Actually, if he had been able to complete his thought, he would only have added "coke and Chocomonsters." But he was interrupted.

Sorgo, of course, "heard" it first, and reacted instantly. The other Carisians heard it too. Tommy sort of heard it. For him, it was more like an adult talking over you when you're at the dinner table. Everyone went silent just to make sure they were "hearing" Commander Thren correctly.

"All members of Earth Station 3PS-204. Please prepare for standard, non-emergency departure from this station. Arnul, you will execute emergency lock-out immediately."

The crew then "heard" Arnul's thoughts coming through, *"Medical teams, please report to your station. We have an emergency. Glefon has been seriously injured."*

Sorgo was already at the companionway door, when Tommy called, "Sorgo, did I understand right? Was that something about Glefon injured?" Sorgo did not turn around, *"Yes, Tommy, I'm afraid so."*

Tommy bounded up from the cushion and caught up to Sorgo just as the pencil thin red line scanned across to reveal the passageway. Tommy was not entirely recovered from his own operation, so those few quick steps made his breathing come heavily and unevenly. Gulping to catch his breath, Tommy struggled, "Sorgo, what happened to him? How is she... is she going to be all right?" Glefon was Tommy's special friend. After all, Glefon and Sorgo did rescue him that awful night. Sure, Glefon was a bit weird. The way she talked and all. But, Glefon was...well, just different...and special.

"I don't know, Tommy," was all the Sorgo managed.

That wasn't good enough. Why doesn't Sorgo just ask. He had to know...now. But, how? He had never done this before - transfer thoughts over a long distance. His friends were always within earshot. This time it had to be through walls, down long corridors, and into the medical facility. He had to do it. He just had to know. He started to think about what he wanted to say. He picked the easiest words and then saw them, each word, each letter in his mind. He mentally typed the words across his mind. Then he focused on each word. He made himself concentrate even as he walked. He screwed his eyes shut and pursed his lips. He thought Sharma's name over and over again and forced the message out of his mind over to Sharma. *"Sharma, this is Tommy. How is Glefon?"*

Tommy was shocked and a little pleased with himself when he got a response, but his concern for Glefon postponed any celebration. *"Tommy, Glefon is gravely injured. Would you please come along to the medical facility as well?"* Sharma replied. Sharma was speaking directly to him! It worked!

Tommy forced a reply, *"I'm coming, Sharma."*

When Sorgo, Tommy and the medical team lead by Tosh entered the room, they saw both Sharma and Commander Thren at the table where Glefon lay. She was lying on her side, curled in a ball and partly covered by a shining silver-gray blanket. Her skin was a strange greenish colour which Tommy could easily see even though everything on the Earth Station seemed to be a shade of gray. The medical teams went silently and immediately to their consoles. Within moments the Mass Accelerator Coupler was activated and the group stood amidst a sea of winking and blinking lights.

Tommy did not ask permission, but slowly went over to Glefon whose eyes were closed. Tommy noticed that she did not appear to be breathing. He could see a hole in Glefon's chest. He turned to look at both Sharma and the Commander. "Sharma, Commander Thren. What happened to Glefon?" Tommy couldn't bother to send his thoughts, because he was struggling with tears. How could this be? His friend Glefon looked as if she were dying. How could he lose a friend he had just made?

The Commander spoke first, *"Glefon was on the Outside carrying on her usual science duties. Apparently, she and her partner were seen by one of your people and was then struck by a projectile fired by a Steven Barker. It would appear judging by his thought projections, that Mr. Barker was very frightened and felt as if Glefon's gesture of peace was a threat."*

Tommy's eyes were streaming with tears. His own people had done this! How could they! Tommy was so angry that he could hardly get the words out between trying to gulp back the tears, "They...shot him? Those stupid, stupid people shot Glefon. Why, Commander Thren. Glefon wasn't going to hurt them? Then why did they do it" Tommy kept on shouting, crying, and raging at his own people. He had been safe here with the gentle Carisians for some time now. He had almost forgotten about home. Well, almost, except his Mom and Dad, of course. But the rest of them. He couldn't care if he ever saw them again. And now they were back in his life. "First they hurt me, now they hurt my friends," he screamed.

For Carisians a question always warrants a reply. Tommy had asked "Why". Commander Thren was now about to change Tommy's life with the answer.

"Tommy, you mustn't be so hard on your people. They were searching for you. I'm afraid they think we are holding you against your will. We have monitored their transmissions. They are using the word 'kidnap'".

Tommy's face froze in a mask of shock. For a moment it was hard for him to take a breath. His throat went dry and he began shaking his head from side to side. "No, this can't be happening...this can't be happening," he began repeating over and over. His chest began to heave. He tried to take deep breaths. He felt as if he were suffocating. He couldn't get the words out. *"Here against my will? Kidnapped?"* he suddenly screamed in his mind almost as if he were projecting his thoughts to the Earth people. He cried out hoping that they would hear him on the Outside, "I haven't been kidnapped. Do you understand? I'm not here against my will. I'm here with my friends, with people who don't care what I look like. And, I'm...I'm happy, do you hear...I'm happy."

Tommy turned to look at Glefon who seemed to be getting worse by the moment. He walked with shoulders hunched forward over to the still Carisian and said softly aloud and in his mind, "*It's my fault. All of this is my fault. I'm sorry, Glefon. I'm so sorry.*"

Commander Thren stepped toward Tommy and gently touched Tommy who instantly felt the calmness running through him. Yes, he was still angry but suddenly he didn't feel like screaming any longer. The Commander sent a thought to the troubled boy, "*Tommy, it's not your fault. No one is at fault. Everyone is doing what they think is right.*"

Tommy turned to the Commander and spoke directly to him. Another thought flashed in his mind. Somehow, he knew who the Commander was. Maybe they didn't all look alike, or maybe, it was something else. "Commander Thren, couldn't we get a message to the Outside to tell them I'm not here. Tell them I'm in Dallas, Texas, or someplace far away."

The Commander understood what the boy was trying to do. "*I'm afraid not, Tommy. Carisians cannot lie. I think that the only choice for us now is to see to Glefon and then to leave the Earth Station as soon as we can."*

Tommy was devastated. He was happy here. He had found new friends and a new life. Perhaps a very different life, but he knew that he was accepted here. No one shrunk away from him because of his face. In fact, he hadn't even thought about his face in so long. Everything seemed like, well, normal. But now, all that was about to change. His friends had been frightened by his own people. There was no telling what would happen if they ever got in the Earth Station. What would happen to him? Where would he go? Back home? No! Never! Well, I'll just leave with my friends. I'll go to Carisor and live with Sorgo, Glefon, Tosh, Lef and all the others. Maybe, Commander Thren would take me to on his next mission. All these thoughts were whirling around in his head...and he knew that everyone was "listening", but he didn't care. *"They're my friends and I trust them,"* he thought very deliberately, hoping that they would hear that.

Before Tommy could continue his thoughts, Sharma came over and looked into Tommy's eyes. *"Tommy, we have a problem and I believe only you can help."*

"I'll do anything to help Glefon," Tommy responded very resolutely.

Sharma gently eased Glefon on to her back. Tommy's eyes widened as he thought he actually <u>heard with his ears</u> a whimper of pain come from Glefon. Sharma gestured for Tommy to come stand next to him. *"Tosh, please commence Thoron scan and project on my overhead monitor for Tommy and myself."*

Instantly, from above the table where Glefon lay, a greenish-blue light appeared and scanned slowly across Glefon, stopping momentarily at her chest wound. At the console at the head of the bed, what looked like an X-ray appeared on the screen. *"Hold, please, and maximise,"* Sharma ordered.

"There, Tommy, can you see it? That is the projectile which entered Glefon"

"You mean the bullet," Tommy said harshly.

"Bullet. Yes, bullet," Sharma repeated trying to accustom himself to this strange word.

"Can't you take it out, Sharma?" Tommy asked simply. "They do things like surgery on the Outside; why not here?" Gesturing to the Mass Accelerator Coupler, Tommy said, "Just put her in that thing you put me into it. It worked for me, didn't it?"

Time was running out for Glefon but Sharma had to use a precious few moments to bring Tommy along. *"The Mass Accelerator Coupler is a fusion device. It cannot remove foreign bodies. It can only regenerate and repair tissue. And in this case, the foreign body is made of a substance that is very dangerous to Carisians. I believe you call it Lead. We cannot come near to this substance even with instruments in order remove the project...the bullet, unless...."*

Tommy did not wait for Sharma to finish. "What...Are you telling me that you can't get the bullet out? Why not?...You can't just let Glefon die."

Sharma suffered the interruption until Tommy had finished venting his anger. Sharma allowed himself a quick observation: *"Interesting, these humans and their emotions. He shows feeling for us."* Then he completed his thought. *"Tommy, can you help us remove the...bullet?"*

"Me?" Tommy's eyes went saucer wide, and he said in a croaked voice. "I'm just a kid - not a surgeon!"

"I'm afraid there's no other way, Tommy. Glefon will most certainly die not only because of the injury caused by the bullet, but also because lead is a deadly poison to Carisians. Lead is not harmful to your people. We must remove the bullet soon if Glefon is to live. I will guide your movements."

Once again, everyone stopped to listen. Tommy looked around the room. All the Carisians were looking at him, waiting for him. Suddenly, he was scared. Sure, Glefon was his friend, but this...operating to remove a bullet. *"Being friends can also be a pain,"* he thought.

The Carisians waited in silence.

"OK, Sharma. I think this is crazy, but if there's no other way... OK, I'll do it." Tommy said both aloud and in his mind. He almost detected a sigh of relief in the room.

"Then let's begin," Sharma said simply.

Tommy bent over close to the Glefon's earhole and whispered, "Glefon. Glefon. It's me, your friend Tommy." Glefon stirred. She moved her head and opened her eyes to look into Tommy's eyes.

"Tommy...friend...I trust...will do your best..." the thoughts trailed away as Glefon closed her eyes.

"Sharma?" Tommy cried out. He was afraid that she had...

"No, Tommy, she is not dead, but we must hurry," Sharma's thoughts broke through as he removed the Protean Disc, the same large M&M shaped device that Sharma had used to put Tommy to sleep

The thought ordered commands by Sharma were flying so fast that Tommy could not understand anything. At a gesture from Sharma, a device appeared from the ceiling which Tommy thought resembled a welder's mask. Sharma gently placed it over Tommy's face. A glove was attached to Tommy's right hand. For a moment Tommy was disoriented until he "heard" Sharma. *"Do not be alarmed, Tommy. The device is a Micro-surgical Enhancer. You are seeing the surgery through an internal array inside your unit. Your fingers operate the probe and retractor elements. Be calm, Tommy, just do as I say. This should only take a moment."*

The heat inside the mask was intense, not from the heat of the instruments but from the tension on Tommy's face. He began to sweat. "Sharma, I'm sweating!", Tommy called out.

"Be calm, Tommy. Now, this is what I want you to do...," Sharma's cool professional voice came through Tommy's headset.

There were no other transmissions except from Sharma to Tommy. There could be no interference from any stray thought waves. Commander Thren observed the proceedings standing alone by the passageway. He watched with amazement as the young boy performed the delicate surgery; and he monitored Tommy's thought waves. Absolute concentration to the task. Tommy was thinking of nothing else at that moment but following Sharma's instructions. And he was doing it for no other reason than to save his friend Glefon. These Earth people were indeed curious. At one moment, dangerous and unpredictable. The next, generous and self-less. The Commander wondered how these people could live with such extreme contradictions.

Sharma continued the steady flow of inch by inch instructions to Tommy. He never lost his patience even after several attempts by Tommy to position the probe at the hole in Glefon's chest failed, leaving Tommy frustrated and yelling into his visor, "Sharma, I can't do it!"

*"You **can** do it Tommy. Be calm. Close your eyes for a moment. Rest. Do not concentrate so much on your fingers. Let your mind guide your fingers,"* Sharma replied evenly. *"Try again, Tommy. You will succeed."*

Rather than walk the probe over to the spot on Glefon's chest, Tommy tried to throw the probe from a fixed point to the hole. It was much like throwing a basketball, he thought. Keep your eye on the basket, then you just hook the ball into the air, and....

Sharma was listening to Tommy's basketball analogy and was about to suggest something a bit more scientific, when -

"There...I got it, I got it! Sharma, the probe is in the hole!" Tommy cried out and jumped up almost losing the probe.

"*Well, done, Tommy,*" was the closest that Sharma would come to both an exclamation and excitement. "*Now, simply position the retractor element alongside the probe. Yes, that's it. Hold there for a moment, Tommy.*" Sharma gestured over to Tosh who was monitoring the operation displayed on one of the screens. "*Tosh, try to lower probe and retractor to the projectile...the bullet,*" Sharma ordered.

Beads of sweat dripped into Tommy's eyes and it stung so that he could hardly see. His head was pounding from the concentration and his throat was so parched he could hardly manage a swallow. He shrugged his shoulders to relieve the tension in his back. Although it had only been a matter of a few minutes, he felt as if he had been standing there for hours.

"*Tommy, we are ready for you to retrieve...the bullet,*" Sharma transferred to Tommy.

Tommy was startled and shook for a second and then responded wearily, "Uh, yea, Sharma, I'm ready."

Just as Sharma was about to resume the surgery, Commander Thren "spoke" to Tommy, "*You are doing well, Tommy, you are doing very well. Not much longer.*"

Tommy turned and was about to acknowledge the Commander, grateful for the kind word, but Sharma prevented any further discussion. "*Tommy, the retractor is in place and as close as we can come to the bullet. You must maneuver the retractor and the probe together for the remainder of the distance to the bullet.*"

"OK," was all that Tommy could manage.

After a few more tense moments, both the probe and retractor elements were touching the bullet, and Sharma was sending thought instructions to Tommy on how to operate the retractor to capture the bullet and remove it from Glefon.

"Got it, Sharma. I've got the bullet."

"*Remove it slowly and after you have cleared the hole deposit the bullet in the case which you will see in your visual display,*" Sharma responded.

As Tommy pulled the retractor element out of Glefon, he dropped the bullet on the floor when he lost his concentration because of stinging sweat in his eyes, fatigue and relief. "OOPS," he said sheepishly as he watched the bullet roll toward the Carisians who calmly but quickly glided out of harm's way.

Tommy quickly lifted the visor, pulled off the glove and went to retrieve the bullet which he then put in the glass tray suspended over Glefon's bed. Instantly, the tray closed and retracted into the ceiling. Immediately, Sharma walked over and picked up the helmet Tommy had been wearing and placed it on his head. Within moments, the operation was proceeding with all team members at Glefon's bedside or at the monitors. All Tommy could do now was stand aside and watch. As he stood waiting, he began to tremble all over. It was now beginning to dawn on him what he had just done. He had performed an operation, and on a Carisian no less! What would the other kids think!

The Commander stepped up to Tommy and sent a thought. *"Tommy, we are very grateful for your help. If you had not been here, Glefon would surely have died. You saved her life. Thank you."*

Just as he was about to send a thought back, Tommy could see the medical team carrying Glefon to the Mass Accelerator Coupler. As tired as he was, Tommy felt he had to respond to this man as a Carisian, *"Sir, Glefon is my friend, and she did save **my** life...and I guess, I owed it to her seeing as my people were the ones who tried to kill her."* Tommy thought to Commander Thren.

Sharma walked over to the Commander and Tommy. He nodded his head to each of them in turn - the Carisian sign of respect. *"Commander. Tommy. Glefon will make a full recovery. Thank you for your help, Tommy. We could not have done it without you."* Sharma was a Carisian of fewer words than most of his people, but he had just paid Tommy a compliment. Tommy nodded a sign of respect in return.

They didn't so much hear it as they felt it. It was a rumble, a deep ominous sound that enveloped them in waves and sent waves of fear through the Earth Station. It wasn't thunder. As they looked around them, they didn't have long to wait to learn the source.

"Commander Thren. This is Arnul. May I ask you to come to the Control Center. The Earth people are using an explosive device at the entrance."

Then there was another rumble.

CHAPTER 33

From the air, the area in and above the ravine looked more like a war zone. Sheriff's deputies had erected barricades on the road; and the ravine floor was crawling, literally at times, with the state police forensics unit, swat unit, deputy sheriffs and volunteers.

"Ready," Deputy White called into the field phone.

"Fire," came the reply from Sheriff Kanter. In an instant, the winter air was shattered by a thunderous bang sending a cloud of dirt, stones and dead wood flying into the air. The ground shook for a moment, and the echo crashed again and again against the ravine walls making it sound as if there were ten explosions.

State Police Lieutenant Lloyd Barton had hunkered down with his SWAT team behind large boulders. For a moment, the sounds brought back the nightmare of a war he endured in Vietnam, crouched then as now listening and feeling the explosions erupting all around him. He turned to look at his team. They're so young. He felt more like a father than a SWAT leader. They were OK.

Lieutenant Barton was the first to stand up as the dust began to settle. He met Deputy White walking over to another location about 100 yards away where a man was hunched over an instrument and peeling paper from a print out. It was Professor Jim Curtin, a seismologist from the University and a member of the State Police Forensics Unit.

"What have you got," asked the lieutenant.

"The returns indicate that there is a honeycomb of narrow passages down there. Strange, though, there's something else. See here?" the professor said running his finger along a portion of the lines. "See these lines? These indicate a hollow under the ground, but the return is... well,...almost muffled. It's as if there's something lining the walls."

"Could it be water," the lieutenant asked.

"No, don't think so. The wave pattern would be different. No, it's definitely not water, but I can tell you this, there's a honeycomb of tunnels and caves under here. And I don't think it's natural," the Professor looked gravely at both men.

The Sheriff had come over in time to overhear the professor's last statement. "But, Professor, that doesn't square with the thermal imaging photographs I received from the Air Force."

"Well, it probably wouldn't Sheriff," the Professor responded as if speaking to a student. "Thermal images can only detect heat returns from structures which are fairly close to the surface. What we have under here is very, very deep and very extensive, and there's something else...There's a pattern to these structures." "Look," he said as he traced his fingers along a weave of lines, "there's a logical pattern here - too logical to be created by nature. What we have here is man-made." And then he added, "Or made by some other intelligent source."

CHAPTER 34

The explosions continued sending sound waves rippling through the Earth Station. In the control room, Commander Thren was "listening" to Arnul's thought report.

"Earth people possess nuclear weapons, and other low yield explosive devices capable of penetrating the Plasma Light Shield. However, they were detonating very low-level explosive devices. My conclusion is that they are taking seismographic soundings, and profiling by means of sound wave detection equipment. Their systems are antiquated but sufficient to disclose our presence."

"Are preparations underway for departure of the Earth Station? the Commander enquired.

"Yes, Commander. All systems are being de-activated except those which relate to the medical treatment facility," Arnul responded. She then added, *"We have received a communication from Commander Kron. He will reach this galaxy in 3 earth days and take up a stationary orbit around Earth. He will contact us at that time to arrange for transfer."*

"Thank you, Arnul. Please keep me informed of all further activity by the Earth people." the Commander ordered. As he turned to leave, Arnul sensed the Commander's thoughts. She knew that the Commander had been

struggling for some time with a difficult decision regarding Tommy. It was a decision which would one the hand change Tommy's life, but on the other defy the directive of the Council of the All Wise prohibiting intervention in the affairs of the Earth people. The others on Earth Station 3PS 204 also knew, of course, but because Carisians were a very proper race of people, no one would ever discuss the matter with the Commander. However, the time was growing short and Commander Kron would soon arrive. There was no more time to stand on Carisian sense of propriety or even on status and rank. Arnul decided to ask the Commander directly.

"Commander, do you think Sharma will be able to complete an operation on Tommy before we leave?"

For a long moment, Thren did not respond. Arnul had stepped outside of all the rules of Carisian behaviour. He turned to face her, although he didn't have to. *"I don't know."* The Commander turned and as he stepped toward the Plasma Light Shield scanner that opened the passageway, he added, *"Thank you, Arnul, for understanding."* He then disappeared into the passageway and the scanner sealed the Control Room leaving Arnul to her own thoughts.

* * *

The Commander entered the medical facility to find all the Carisians were standing around Glefon's bed each with the palm of their hands resting on Glefon, each projecting the inner warmth and peace that Carisians were capable of producing. Sharma, Sorgo and Tommy were standing at the head of the bed, also touching Glefon. Tommy was holding Glefon's delicate right hand in his, rubbing the back of her hand.

Sharma sensed the return of the Commander Thren to the facility before he actually saw him, and he had also "heard" the conversation between Arnul and the Commander. Without waiting for what he knew would be Commander Thren's questions, Sharma responded, *"Commander, as you can see, Glefon is healed and will be ready for transfer to Commander Kron's ship. As far as Tommy is concerned, I am prepared to perform the surgery should you request and, of course, should he desire it."*

Sorgo looked up at both the Commander and Sharma. Tommy was still looking intensely at Glefon, waiting for Glefon to open her eyes.

"Thank you, Sharma," was all the Commander could manage. Time was running out fast for the Carisians. Although the rumbles from Outside had stopped, the Commander knew that it was only a matter of time before the Earth people discovered the Earth Station and would force an entry. But there was no telling how long it would take. This could get ugly.

Commander Thren walked over to Tommy in order to make it easier for Tommy to "hear" what he was about to say. *"Tommy, this is Commander Thren."*

Tommy startled and looked up. The thought that he had just received from Commander Thren came in as clearly as if he heard them with his ears. "Oh, hello, sir,

"Tommy said aloud. He then said the same in his thoughts, although it came more slowly.

If Carisians could smile, the Commander would have. *"Thank you, Tommy. You have made great progress in communicating with us by thought transfer and we appreciate your efforts, but I think it would be easier in this conversation if you responded orally."*

This sounded serious to Tommy. First the shooting of Glefon, then the rumbles, and then the order to evacuate the Earth Station. He, too, could almost sense what the Commander was going to say. Almost, but not quite. "Yes, sir," Tommy responded aloud.

"As you know Tommy, we must leave your planet in view of everything that has happened. I expect that we should be leaving in about three of your Earth days. Your thoughts have told me that you would like to leave with us, but that is not possible...for many reasons," the Commander said very directly but was interrupted before he could continue.

"But, sir, I **can** come with you. I could learn about Carisian ways. Sorgo, and Glefon when she gets better, will teach me things I need to know, and I don't eat much, and I won't get in the way...and, well, look at me how can I stay here when all people see is a "snake face"? Tommy blurted out as tears began to well in his eyes. *Go back, how could he? Where would he go? No, I'm not going back home!* I hate them all! Tommy's thoughts came in a rush. He released Glefon's hand and turned to face the Commander.

The Commander read Tommy's thoughts and then realized that Tommy deserved a fuller explanation and to be treated not like a child but like...a Carisian. *"Tommy,"* he began again, *"We do not have the experience with humans. We do not know how to provide for you as a member of our crew. We do not know how you will react to Encapsulation. That is the process of placing our bodies in a low dynamic state, suspended in a pressurized Magnite solution during the long space flights. Those are the physical dimensions. For you Earth people, there is another element for which we are unprepared - your emotions. We, and you, Tommy, because of your youth have little experience with those. And finally, you will age, Tommy, without ever having contact with your Earth people again...ever."* The Commander thought that this last point may have been too much for the young boy, judging by the strained expression on Tommy's face, but there was no other way. Then, Thren offered, *"Tommy, we think that you really want and need to be with your people,.."*

Tommy was about to interrupt but the Commander raised his hand for Tommy to remain silent. Thren continued, *"...and, we also know that what happened to you made you so angry with your own people that you were willing to risk your life to flee. It is also the reason that you want to leave with us - to continue your flight from the people who hurt you."* The Commander did not wait for Tommy to reply although he could feel the boy's angry thoughts. *"But, I think we might be able to help, Tommy, if you will let us.*

"How?" Tommy said, looking intently into the Commander eyes. Tommy's voice had a harsh, almost bitter edge to it. He was hurt and angry at the Carisians. Now his friends were going to abandon him too.

Thren felt Tommy's anger but ignored it. Time, there was no time. *"Sharma informs me that we can restore your face to its original features. If you wish, we will do this immediately in order that you may be ready to return to your people...to your family, upon our departure."*

"Do you mean that you can make me look the way I used to before the accident?" Tommy asked, but disbelieving. He had been through too much. It was just more plastic surgery, more pain and more failure. No, this was not possible.

This time it was Sharma who "spoke" after picking up Tommy's last thought. *"Yes, Tommy, it is possible."*

"Sharma, you can't make me look like I used to. Look at me. My face is ...well, it's disgusting; it's ugly...and there's nothing that you or anybody can do about it."

Sharma's reply was curious. It almost seemed that Sharma was,...irritated. Unheard of amongst Carisians under any circumstances, but these weren't just any circumstances. *"Tommy, please do not think like an Earth person. You have seen what we have done here; first with you and now with Glefon. Tommy, we* **can** *do it."*

"You can?" True, Tommy had seen what these Carisians could do. Well, why couldn't they give him a new face, he thought.

"No, Tommy, not a **new** face," Sharma said "hearing" Tommy's last thought. "We will **restore** your face to its original condition with its original features."

"But how can you do that? You don't even know what I looked like. I'm not sure that I even remember any more." Tommy said adding a hint of bitterness to the last words.

"We will probe your mind. There, our scan will find the image of yourself before your accident and we will reproduce it. From that, we will recreate your original facial features," Sharma said trying to simplify a procedure which had taken a thousand pel to develop.

"OK, let's say, you **can** make a picture of me, how are you going to get skin and bone. I can't use your Carisian skin. It would look pretty funny on the Outside." Tommy replied sarcastically, but then he hastily added, "Sorry, ...but you know what I mean." He didn't know why he was being such a brat, but he still thought it would be easier for them just to take him with them back to Carisor. That would solve the problem.

"I know what you mean," Sharma sympathized. "But, we already have made skin and bone for you." Sharma had hoped that he wasn't going to have to disclose this, but it was too late for that now.

"What do you mean? Tommy sounded amazed and a little frightened.

"Tommy, the Mass Accelerator Coupler can **restore and replace** tissue. It cannot **regenerate** dead tissue. We discovered *when you were in the Mass Accelerator that your fingers and toes had been completely destroyed. They had to be replaced. And we did."*

Tommy eyes widened and his jaw slowly began to drop open. Then, he quickly looked at his hands. He inspected each finger, turning them, and wiggling them. He put one into his mouth. He bit on the nail. He then looked closer. Yes, there were fingerprints too. "You mean...these are not my fingers...?" Tommy stammered.

"Yes, Tommy, they are your fingers. They're just not your original ones," came Sharma's precise reply.

For a moment, Tommy couldn't say, or even think anything. And then it hit him. *Oh, my God. They had to amputate my fingers and toes!* Tommy kept staring at his fingers. He shook his head trying to get over the shock of what Sharma had just said. He tried wiggling his toes. "You mean you cut them off...I didn't know." Tommy just sat there, staring at his hands. "Hey, why didn't you ask me; why didn't you tell me what you were going to do," Tommy demanded.

"There was no time and it was not necessary for your recovery, but I assure you, Tommy, they are in all respects like the originals."

"Are you sure?" Tommy looked at Sharma from the corner of his eyes as he continued to wiggle his fingers.

"Yes, Tommy, I am quite certain. And now that we have the information in our data banks, we can develop the necessary tissue

for your face...with the same effect as your fingers and toes," Sharma concluded. *"The decision to proceed is yours."*

"Just like the original, Sharma?" Tommy wanted to "hear" Sharma reassure him again

"Yes, Tommy, just like the original."

Tommy knew. He always knew that at some point he would have to return. Sure, it would be cool if he could go off to Carisor for the rest of his life, but he knew it couldn't be. He would have to go back to his own people. Well, if he had to go back, it might as well be as the original Tommy Flagg, not as "snake face". And well, he did sort of miss home, especially his Mom and Dad; his room, and the smell of waffles for breakfast on Saturday morning. If Sharma could make him look like he did before the accident, well, maybe, he might even learn to like his friends again. He thought for the longest time...and he knew that the Carisians were listening. One last thing...

"Sharma, will it hurt?"

"No, Tommy, it will not," Sharma responded quickly.

He couldn't stand the thought of going through life looking like he did. He was so afraid to get his hopes up that the Carisians could do what his doctors at the hospital couldn't do. He couldn't live any longer with the pain, any kind of pain. But, he had seen what the Carisian could do, but he still continued to wiggle his toes and flex his fingers. And he so much wanted to look,... well normal; you know, just like any other kid.

Tommy took in a deep breath, exhaled and said, as he slowly nodded his head, "OK, Sharma, ...I'll do it.... Would you do it, please?"

Sharma placed a reassuring hand on Tommy and said, "*Yes, I would be pleased to and it will turn out well, Tommy. Remember, Carisians never lie;.... nor do your fingers and toes.*" Tommy smiled. Another table was brought alongside Glefon's and as he was about to climb up, Glefon's eyes opened and she turned to Tommy. For an instant, she just looked at Tommy without conveying a thought.

"Glefon!... Glefon, you're OK! I'm so happy to see you," Tommy exclaimed as he bent over and threw his arms around Glefon. Without hesitating he gave her a gentle kiss on the cheek. He didn't notice the cool feel of her Carisian skin on his lips. Glefon was OK and that's all that mattered. Tommy did not "hear" the buzz of Carisian thoughts whirling throughout the Earth Station: "*Unusual display. Evidence of emotions. Warm thoughts passing to Glefon. Curious human reaction. However, pleasant*" were some of the transmissions speeding from Carisian to Carisian.

Glefon's thoughts came slowly, almost haltingly, "*Do not be frightened, Tommy. It is a simple exo-cranio-facial reconstruction procedure.*"

Tommy immediately looked over to Sorgo who looked at Tommy, "*Yes, Tommy, I think Glefon is feeling much better. Glefon is trying to say that you are having a simple operation on your face.*"

Tommy looked back at Glefon, smiled, rolled his eyes back and shook his head. Yes, things are back to normal...almost.

"Are you ready, Tommy?" Sharma enquired.

As Tommy hoisted himself up on the operating table, he looked at Sorgo, Glefon, the Commander and all the other Carisians in the room. He started to receive the warm feelings that all his friends were sending to him - their way of reassuring him, he thought. He looked at Sharma and sent a clear thought-speak. *"Yes, Sharma, I'm ready."*

With that, Sharma gently placed the Protean Disc at Tommy's temple and within seconds, Tommy fell blissfully asleep.

One by one, each of the Carisians in the room came over and placed a hand on Tommy's head and then either left the room or went to a workstation. Thren gave a thought order to Sorgo and Glefon, *"Please stay with Tommy until the end."*

Sorgo replied for both, *"Yes, Commander."*

The Commander approached Tommy who was now deeply asleep and being prepared for the procedure. For a long time, the Commander stood looking down at the young boy with a mix of thoughts and...feelings. For the first time in his life, the Commander had allowed himself to *feel* - a strange mixture of happiness and sadness. It was curious that such an advanced race of people as the Carisians could learn so much from this Earth child.

Carisians had developed into the most intelligent beings in the known galaxies, but it took this boy to make them remember things that they had forced into the recesses of their memories over the millennia - things like feelings and emotions, laughter and, yes, even sadness. The boy felt pain over the cruelty of his friends; the near loss of Glefon and then joy over seeing Glefon alive; and the pleasure he took eating the substance he calls Chocomonsters. Commander Thren knew that his thoughts were being monitored by the others. He did not know that the feelings were also being transmitted. They came across as a garbled, and unspecified jumble- almost like being caught between two badly tuned radio stations. The others picked up the thoughts and at the same time tried to tune into these new and strange transmissions by the Commander. He looked around the room and suddenly, like children caught in the act of misbehavior, all the other Carisians stopped and turned their attentions away.

The Commander thought to everyone and to no one, *"It's quite all right. I understand."*

He took a last look at the Earth child, *"Good-bye, Tommy Flagg. May you live in peace."*

Thren turned to Sharma, *"You know what must be done. I know you will do your best, but take care with him. He is very special. You may proceed."*

"Commander, this is Arnul. The Earth people are trying to break the Plasma Shield."

CHAPTER 35

Sheriff Kanter looked on as the giant Chinook helicopter, known affectionately as the "Jolly Green Giant", with its two enormous rotor blades beat down trees and sent clouds of dirt roiling into the air as it hovered above the ravine. Slowly this giant lowered a strange looking vehicle that had been suspended from the belly of the helicopter. It was half pile driver-half armored personnel carrier. It had the treads of a battle tank, but instead of a gun turret, there was a long drill like apparatus at the front end. This was the Well Head Initiator and Probe vehicle, otherwise known as the "WHIP". With this unusual vehicle, oil exploration companies could quickly and cheaply initiate drilling operations at a known oil resource or probe at possible oil sites without having to construct expensive drilling rigs.

Petrolex, a large oil exploration company, had agreed to lend the vehicle to the Federal Bureau of Investigation and the US Army. Both had been called in to this case by the State Police after the bizarre occurrences at the site, and the discovery of a very sophisticated array of deep underground caves which everyone agreed were made by intelligent beings. Given the depth, it was impossible that an ancient civilization was responsible. And there was no recent record of any excavation or construction.

That left only one thing - an alien civilization. By this time, everyone, except his parents and the Sheriff, had forgotten the fact that Tommy was also traced to this location.

Sheriff Kanter and his team of deputies and volunteers were now largely spectators together with a growing crowd of the news media, representatives of UFO International, and sightseers who detoured to this area. Everyone was hoping for a glimpse of alien space craft...at least that was the rumor.   It did not go unnoticed that a large company of Army Rangers was already in the ravine - with weapons.

Tommy's parents were also in the crowd. They had come not because of rumors and stories of aliens, but rather hopeful that somehow all of this was connected to Tommy and would lead to his discovery. They saw the sheriff who waved them over to him. He positioned himself between both Joanna and Scott and put his arms around them. Shouting above the din of the helicopter, he said, "There's something down there, and those people are going to find it...and they're going to find Tommy in the process. I'm sure of it." He turned them both away from the noise, gusts and other spectators, particularly the press. He said that the investigators were now sure that there was an entrance to the subterranean system which was sealed somehow. With the WHIP vehicle they were going to attempt to break through.

Joanna Flagg was shielding her eyes from the storm kicked up by the giant chopper hovering above them. It sent down wave after wave of powerful gusts of dust and grit stinging their faces like thousands of fine needles. She bent over to the sheriff and yelled into his ear, "What are they going to do? And why are you so sure that Tommy is in there?"

"Call it instinct, call it experience, call it whatever you like, Joanna, but something tells me that all of what's been happening down there and Tommy's disappearance are connected. I don't know how, but it's no coincidence," the Sheriff replied. He thought to himself, "No there weren't hard facts; no positive shreds of evidence to link these events to Tommy's disappearance." Call it a hunch, a suspicion...He couldn't put his finger on it, but he just knew.

Joanna called it intuition. Yes, Tommy was in there. She was sure of it too.

Over his radio, the sheriff heard the WHIP crews positioning the vehicle along the ravine wall, between the spots where Deputy Lou White first saw the thin wires which glowed then melted. It had been decided that as "they were dealing with an unknown force down here", the WHIP vehicle would be operated by remote control.

The helicopter was waved off and within seconds everything went quite. There was no sound but the crackling on the radio.

After several long hours as the late afternoon sun began to lay down long shadows over the White Bluff, the crews signaled that they were ready to begin.

The WHIP crews had set up station about 100 yards from the vehicle. Mark Stiles, affectionately known by such names as "dyno-geek" and "electro-nerd", was a computer genius and the remote operator of WHIP. He sat with a joystick between his legs amidst an array of switches and dials. His TV monitor received transmissions from a camera mounted atop the WHIP. With his communications headset in place, he was plugged in, and ready to go. "Control, this is remote operator. Ready to commence probe," Mark said simply. For Mark Stiles this was fun. A video game come to life with one difference...he got paid to play with it.

The reply came quickly, "This is Control. Stand-by Mark. We're waiting for the Army to confirm that they are in position." Seconds later: "Roger that, Army. OK, Mark, it's all yours."

Like an organist at Sunday service, Mark began pushing buttons, and flipping switches. His TV screen jumped to life and in the distance, he could hear the WHIP's engine growl to life. Within seconds, it became a roar which was deafening to the point where everyone reached for ear protectors to cut out the noise. Mark studied the console. All systems operating normally. It was time to engage the drill probe. He pressed the "Engage" button and the engine rumble was now mixed with a high-pitched whine that reminded everyone within earshot of the same thing: a dentist's drill. Slowly, gently, he pushed his joystick forward. The probe responded as the titanium drill bit into the soft topsoil, and within seconds disappeared.

* * *

"Commander, our sensors show that they Earth people have inserted a mechanical probe near the Plasma Shield," Arnul thought.

"Arnul, fire a Trimedian Pulse at force factor 3," Commander Thren ordered.

"Pulse - 3 - fired...now," Arnul responded immediately as he touched a tall crystal rod at his console.

* * *

Suddenly, there was a deep and ominous moan that welled up from under the ravine. It was more like the sound of a large animal stirred out of sleep, and once disturbed might strike at any moment. The ground began to rock gently with a steady rhythm. Small loose stones began falling into the ravine. As quickly as it started, it suddenly stopped.

One nervous member of the WHIP crew looked at another and asked the WHIP operator quizzically, "Earthquake?" But he only received a shrug for a reply. Mark Stiles was too engrossed in his living video arcade game even to notice. The whine of the drill said Mark was pressing on.

Professor Jim Curtin was in his laboratory when the alarm on the seismograph went off. He walked over to inspect the read out. It showed an earthquake...no, that was no earthquake. He looked more closely at the graph. The waves are too evenly distributed to be an earthquake. It's too focused, too well directed. It was a pulse of energy emanating from one spot...the ravine! ...And then as if in a flash, he knew. "Oh, my God, that's no earthquake, that was deliberate. Someone or something **is** down there!" He ran for his telephone.

* * *

"Commander, sensors show probe activity continuing," Arnul reported.

"Arnul, increase Trimedian Pulse to force factor 6," came the response from Thren.

"Pulse - 6 - fired...now," Arnul touched the crystal rod again.

* * *

Someone - it looked like one of his deputies - was waving to him and motioning with his thumb and pinkie fingers by his ear that he had a telephone call. But as Sheriff Kanter started toward the car, the ground began to shake violently. He stumbled and caught himself before falling. The bridge across the ravine was shaking. People began running in every direction in a panic-stricken attempt to find a safe place.

In the ravine, trees bent and broke at their bases as if an evil and angry hand was shaking them at the crews and the Army Rangers. Stones and fallen tree limbs began to cascade down the ravine sending everyone running for cover. All that is, except the "electro-nerd", Mark Stiles, who was still intently focused on the WHIP controls even though he and his screens were bouncing around. As Mark was rocked back and forth in the tremor, the wire lead to his communication headset had come out of the socket at the transmitter. He was now cut off. He didn't know it, and he really didn't care. He began programming for the next deep probe phase.

Sheriff Kanter reached the deputy's car and took the telephone. "Yea, this is Kanter. Professor Curtin? This better be good."

"Listen, sheriff and don't say a word. Sheriff, those earthquakes you're having now? Well, they're not earthquakes. Trust me. They're gigantic electro-magnetic pulses of some kind. It's beyond anything man made. There's someone down there, Sheriff, and I think they're trying to tell you, no, warn you, not to continue. Sheriff, if they have that kind of power that they can control at will, there's no telling how much power they can generate. I think you should stop right now."

The Sheriff believed the professor. If there were creatures, or whatever controlling these earth tremors, then surely the next one would bring the bridge down killing everyone on the bridge, and would crush the people in the ravine. He thanked the professor and reached for his field phone, and called, "All units, all units, this is Sheriff Kanter. Army, WHIP, FBI. All drilling activities have to stop. I've been informed that what we are experiencing is not an earthquake. It has been caused by intelligent beings in the area. I repeat cease drilling, immediately!"

But the Sheriff could still hear the whining of the drill. He screamed into the phone, "WHIP crew, stop the drilling NOW!"

Mark Stiles, the "dyno-geek" engaged the secondary and deep probe drivers. And as he did so, it touched the Plasma Shield. In the blink of the eye, the WHIP vehicle was engulfed by a thunderous explosion sending a huge fireball into the sky. It rocked the ravine; and within moments, the once rugged looking vehicle was reduced to a pile of smoldering and twisted metal.

* * *

All the Carisians felt the vibration in the Earth Station. Although they never let themselves succumb to fear, they knew the situation was dangerous and with that explosion, it was now life threatening. They had been discovered.

"Commander, the Earth people's probe came in contact with the Plasma Shield and was completely destroyed," Arnul made his report slowly this time, aware of the immediate danger they now faced..

"Was their any harm or loss of any lives," came the Commander's reply.

"Please wait, Commander, I will monitor their communications," Arnul offered. Without waiting for Arnul to complete the scan of the frequencies, the Commander enquired, *"And the Plasma Shield?"*

"The Shield is intact, Commander, but I am afraid that the Earth people are now convinced of our presence...Communications indicate only minor injuries."

Arnul sensed Thren's next question before he asked it. Arnul responded, *"Commander Kron has signaled that he has entered Earth's galaxy. He has monitored events and indicates that he will be ready for an emergency evacuation. He has requested your instructions."*

In the Medical Facility, Sharma looked up as he felt the vibrations from the explosions shake his hands. He stopped the probe insertion procedure and waited. If he could allow himself to feel irritation, he would have. The tension was building among the staff. Sharma sent a terse thought order for calm during this delicate stage of Tommy's operation. He began again. The room fell "silent". The technicians held their breaths as they watched Sharma's brilliant surgical technique on their monitors. Slowly, ever so slowly, Sharma inserted the final hair thin sensor of the Genarian mind probe behind Tommy's eye. The probe had just settled in place when another shock wave, this time larger and longer than the first, rolled through the Facility. For the first time, Sharma allowed himself to think about the possibility of not completing the operation in time...and the effect that it would have on the little Earth boy lying in front of him. He promised Tommy that all would be well. It was a promise and Carisians always, always kept their promises.

"Tosh, please activate the Genar scanner and prepare to record. Image projection when you are ready," Sharma ordered.

The technicians glided through the maze of instruments. It all resembled a well-choreographed ballet. "No one "spoke". Crystals glimmered and monitors blinked in a blaze of colors. After a few moments, the large room went pitch dark except for the eerie glow around Sharma who was hunched over staring intently into Tommy's face.

Suddenly, a shaft of laser light pierced the darkness and came to a point in the middle of the room. The beam then broke up and began flickering into a rainbow of a thousand subtle colors. Sharma and the technicians turned and watched intently as the multi-colored beams of light began forming themselves into a vague image. What appeared to be a face began to take shape, disappeared, then began to form again. The process repeated itself several times, but there was no clear image of Tommy's face.

"Tosh?" Sharma thought to his senior technician as he watched the image struggling to form itself. *"Is there a problem?"*

"All systems are within normal ranges," Tosh replied as he continued to watch the holographic image alternatively

form a loose shape then break up into changing weaves of threads of light.

Sharma was very concerned. Time was fast disappearing. There was no telling what would happen with the next explosions which he knew would come. His previous patients were Carisians, including children. Could it be that the Genar scan would not work on the brains of Earth creatures with their range of complex and often conflicting emotions. *"Or could it be that Earth children generally have no strong memories of themselves as individuals? Or has Tommy put up a very strong memory block because of the emotions raised by remembering the way he looked prior to his accident?"* Sharma continued to think "out loud".

Sharma's thoughts were suddenly interrupted. *"Sharma, this is Commander Thren. Please advise the status of Tommy."*

Sharma hesitated for a moment; then said, *"I'm afraid, Commander, we are experiencing difficulty in reconstructing Tommy's mental image of himself. I do not know whether the problem is with the Genar scanner or Tommy's emotional resistance to releasing an image of himself."*

The Commander shot back his thought question. *"Can he be ready for transport tonight, Sharma?"*

"No, Commander, we will not be able to complete the procedure as the situation stands presently." Sharma waited for a reply. But this time, there was long silence. He could not have prepared himself for what he heard.

After thinking to himself for several long moments, the Commander ordered. *"All personnel, this is Commander Thren. Would anyone who spoke with Tommy please assemble in the Medical Facility immediately. I will be there in a moment."*

The Commander turned to Arnul who was waiting for the orders she knew would come. *"Arnul, please initiate emergency withdrawal procedures. I want this Earth Station decommissioned and destroyed. Crew should be prepared to depart on my order. And one last thing, Arnul. Kindly open a high gain Sorex-9 frequency. I wish to make a Torlant Network Communication to Commander Kron and to Carisor. Thank you, Arnul."*

With that, Arnul left the Control Room. It was clear to Arnul that the Commander intended to leave immediately under the cover of darkness. The situation was out of control and lives - theirs as well as the Earth people - were now in grave danger. A night extraction from the Earth Station would be risky, at the very least, and could prove catastrophic. Arnul's first stop was the medical facility - and Tommy.

* * *

The beauty of the ravine had been ravaged by two man-made tremors and the ball of fire that turned the WHIP to cinders. A forest fire had broken out and was threatening to spread. Smoke jumpers, fire fighters, police, FBI agents and WHIP crews were running in every direction following urgent, sometimes angry commands over two-way radios. Fire equipment now mixed in the jumble of police cars, WHIP crew vans, and ambulances and helicopters evacuating the wounded. This wasn't just a disaster, this was a **war zone**.

And like any war zone, there were the fighters. There were Army Rangers, now reinforced by local National Guard armored vehicles and several battle tanks. Every few minutes a squadron of F-18's thundered overhead flying in random patterns like angry bees around a disturbed hive.

This was no longer about a search for a missing boy, Tommy Flagg. It was now a national security alert. The nation had been "invaded" and the invaders whoever or whatever they were had clearly demonstrated that their intentions were hostile.

"No, General, I disagree. I don't think their intentions are hostile." Professor Curtin spoke calmly but with firm conviction. General Al Wallace who was designated the Joint Task Force leader of this operation, now code named "StarBright", chaired the angry meeting.

Search operations had stopped for the night. Wounded needed to be evacuated, the firefighting teams needed time to stop the fire before it climbed out of the ravine, and the General needed time to regroup for his own attack, to bring the battle back to the invaders. But first the meeting.

It was 2 o'clock in the morning. They had been meeting now for six long and very tense hours. Each side was still blaming the other for miscommunications; lack of communication; lack of preparation; lack of leadership; and on and on. Shouts and finger pointing punctuated the air. He had said nothing for the entire meeting. But it was the Professor's comment, "I don't think their intentions are hostile" that stopped the conversation instantly. All eyes turned on him.

The Professor was shaking his head. He spoke slowly and very deliberately; more for emphasis. "No, General, they're not hostile. I think that they were warning us off the site. First, they tried a small pulse and then a larger one. I think if they wanted to, they could have killed us all in an instant."

General Wallace was almost grateful for the Professor's comments. At least everyone had stopped shouting and talking at the same time. If nothing else, Professor Curtin had set himself up as the lightening rod. "If that's so, Professor," the General challenged, "Then how do you account for the explosion."

"I don't know, General, but I'll bet that your WHIP device was destroyed when it accidentally hit something - like stepping on a land mine or touching an electrified fence." The Professor waited for the General, anyone, to say something. When no one did, he offered his own ominous warning, "General, based on my seismographic analysis, I think that if these people wanted to, they could probably call out fire power that you could only dream about."

Then there was silence.

General Wallace listened attentively with his hands prayerfully folded at his lips, staring coldly ahead of him. He was a giant of a man. At six feet, six inches and 320 pounds, he dominated the other end of the table. He was more of a menacing presence. His wolfish eyes were assessing each person seated around the table. He waited, as the silence grew longer.

The silence had become uncomfortable for all but the General. Feet were shuffling, and muted coughs broke out. Eyes were darting about, hoping for someone to say something.

Still he waited. The silence was unbearable. Everyone waited for the General to speak.

General Wallace began to speak. It was like the thunder you hear in the distance from an approaching storm. "These beings have shown their intentions. They are hostile. We can't have these people" – he corrected himself, "these creatures, on this planet with that kind of firepower and the willingness to use it at their own discretion just to send a message. If this is how they communicate, they are a clear and present danger to this country, to the world." He paused as if he wanted to make a larger case, but the pause was not for effect but more to complete his own thoughts: Yes, he could have raised the disappearance of the child, Tommy Flagg, in this very spot. No, they never sent a message of peace. Just two earthquakes that caused damage and injury. Yes, these were definitely hostiles. His looked at the assembled attendees, alternately at each one of them. Then, he said it.

"I have been authorized by the President of the United States to use a low-yield underground nuclear device to break open the caves."

The silence turned to wide-eyed shock and was broken by a gasp. Several faces went ashen. They **couldn't** utter a sound. Now, the General had neither the time nor the inclination to discuss the matter any further. The nation was in peril, and all these people could do was to argue about who was responsible. Well, they had their time to talk and to whine, but now it was time to act. This was a matter of national and global security. He signaled to an aide who distributed a large brown envelope to each person in the room, except Professor Curtin. Each envelope was sealed with a wide tape, and had the particular person's name typed in bold print. Stamped in large black letters on both sides was "**TOP SECRET**".

"Gentlemen, each of you on this "StarBright" team has been given a particular assignment. Kindly take your envelope to a private area, and read the material. Do not share it with anyone else but those of us here in the room. Report back here in one hour." For a moment, no one moved. He cast a hard glance around the room, and quickly everyone rose to leave. He dismissed Professor Curtin with a simple directive, "Thank you, Professor, you may leave."

But it wasn't quite that easy. The Professor was not about to give up. "General, you can't be serious! A nuclear device?"

The General said nothing. The others delayed their leaving; some took their seats again waiting, hoping, perhaps for a different outcome.

The Professor began again; this time he was pleading. "General, don't you understand? Those people under the ravine **made** the earth tremors. They controlled the intensity. I have proof, General. This is like sending a blowgun against cannons. They have an enormous power down there. When, or if, you breach their site, do you think that they are just going to let you walk in? They could retaliate with ten, twenty...a hundred times your nuclear device. Don't you see? They've warned us. They want to be left alone. There is an alternative, General. We could send simple sonar pulses back down, pulses sequenced to convey a message like code. We have to establish some communication with these people to let them know we mean them no harm. Bombing them is not the answer."

The General nodded to his aide who went over to the Professor and stood over him...waiting. The fear was written over Professor Curtin's face as he looked wildly around the room. "Don't you agree? Any of you? What you are about to do is madness?"

Several people turned away. Some just looked down at their shoes. But, no one said anything.

"Thank you, Professor," the General said again. Curtin got up and left the room.

"Gentlemen, there isn't much time. Detonation will be at 9:00 PM tomorrow night."

* * *

When he entered the medical facility, the Commander saw about fifty of Tommy's new Carisian friends assembled in a loose formation off to the left of the room awaiting his direction. There was Sorgo, and Glefon, at the head of the formation, of course. Standing in the front ranks was Arthen, the communications specialist who monitored all of Tommy's favorite TV programs, especially the baseball play-offs; Rol, the chemist who to Tommy's delight and amazement could produce an unlimited supply of Chocomonsters, hamburgers and pizza; and Tel, the language synthesizer and the youngest of the Carisian team who never did get an answer to the origin of the expression, "Yabba Dabba Do". There were the others. All had been touched by the little boy's infectious laughter, frankness and unusual taste in nourishment. But it was Commander Thren who was perhaps the most affected. Tommy had stirred feelings - something he and his fellow Carisians had been taught to suppress, to ignore and to avoid. Feelings. It had touched the members of the Carisian team at 3PS 204, and they knew they would never be the same. This little earthling had brought something into their lives that was unsettling, but at the same time... Neither the

210

Commander nor any of the Carisians could complete that thought. It was strange.

Commander Thren noted quickly that except for the thought transfers between Sharma at the operating table and Tosh at the controls of the Genar Scanner, the room was absolutely "silent". In the middle of the room, strands of colored lights cascaded from the darkness above as the Genar Scanner repeatedly attempted in vain to unlock Tommy's deep and painful resistance to producing an image of himself before his accident. Time after time, a holographic picture of Tommy's face flickered unsteadily, formed for a brief moment, then shattered into a thousand little bits. It was much like dumping pieces of a puzzle in a box and then shaking them up for good measure.

Tommy's face contorted as he fought the Genar Scan's probe deeper into the secret places where Tommy had hidden the pain of the accident. But struggle as he might, he could not resist the continuous and tenacious intrusion of the scanner as it searched every corner, every recess looking for an image, the image of Tommy before the accident.

Deeper and deeper. Tommy felt again the searing heat on his face, the fire in his lungs and the pain from the operations.

Deeper. He felt a different pain -- the pain of seeing his face, and the jeers from his classmates in school. He heard them taunting him again, "Snakeface...snakeface", over and over. His body twisted and arched, his head shook violently from side to side.

Deeper still. The little boy saw his demons again - fear and death. Tommy's face and body were drenched with sweat as he battled both the Genar Scanner and the monsters it generated.

Commander Thren watched the recurring collage of images appear and disappear over and over again. The fleeting image of a tussled haired earthling engulfed in flame, only to reappear as a Carisian look-alike; and then dissolve into a chaotic mass of light beams hovering in the air much like a jumble of static lines on a TV set. He suddenly turned to the group and without observing the time honored Carisian courtesies, the Commander ordered, *"Form a circle around him. I want each of you to join hands. Those of you closest to him place your hands on him and focus your energies. Our combined strength should give him the calm and courage he needs to confront this horrible event in his life and then to recreate the past image of himself."*

Slowly they glided toward Tommy's bed and as they did so joined their bony hands and directed their dark eyes on the terrified little boy struggling in vain. Within moments, the air in the medical facility began to glow -- first a pale yellow that then turned into a deep warm orange -- much the same as the glow at sunset when the sun seems to linger for that one last moment above the horizon before darkness.

The glow reflected off each of the Carisians and seemed to transform their pallid metallic skins into a lustrous red satin. The powerful forces emanating from the Carisians penetrated Tommy's skin and combined with his entire being. His body glowed like a firefly on a summer's night.   He stopped struggling; and for a moment opened his eyes. He turned slowly almost painfully to look at the source of this wondrous feeling. He managed a feeble smile as he saw them.

Then he **felt** them, felt them inside of himself.

They were there with him. Sorgo, Glefon, Tosh, the Commander, and yes, even Sharma. They were all holding his hand it seemed. They were with him in the bus, and stayed with him during the fire. They were his friends -- they wouldn't abandon him.

Yes, and there they were again in the hospital with Doctor Joe and his Mom and Dad.

He could actually hear Sorgo speaking , "It will be all right, Tommy, do not be afraid any longer. We're your friends -- always.

Tommy now could see Doctor Joe and Nurse Gail Franklin in the hospital at his bedside. He could hear Doctor Joe speaking to him, "Well, Tommy, if you're ready, we'll take off your bandages for a moment, so you can see yourself. Before I do, Tommy, I want you to know that it will probably look bad to you. You won't look like you did before your face was burned. You've got scars and your face and neck are still very raw from the burns. And that's not all. You've lost most of your hair, although that will grow back in a matter of a few weeks? We've done everything we can thus far, Tommy. I'm not going to give up on trying to get you back to normal. The rest of it is up to you...Ready?"

And when Doctor Joe cut the bandages and gave Tommy the mirror – suddenly, they were all there – Mom, Dad, Doctor Joe, Gail, Sorgo, Glefon, the Commander - standing around the bed waiting. And... there he was... good as new! "See everyone, I knew it would turn out like this. See, not a mark on my face!"

Tommy turned back, and closed his eyes. He could not see the Genar Scanner projecting a perfect image of his face floating in the middle of the room. The Carisians turned to look, and there he was, for all the world to see -- the smiling face of Tommy Flagg. He had come back. **He was ready now**.

The room darkened again as each Carisian went about the final preparations. The scanner took the image of the smiling boy, and while slowly rotating it, reduced it to three dimensional grid lines floating in space. Eyes, ears, nose, chin and cheeks were transformed into a myriad of intersecting grid lines. The Genar Scanner silently recorded the data sending instructions to the Mass Accelerator Coupler.

The Commander lingered for a few moments in the medical facility. As he looked down at Tommy now lying peacefully on the operating table being readied for surgery, the strange thing occurred. Again, he experienced it...a feeling. It was not the first time that such a thing had occurred when he was around this young earth child, but this time it was unmistakable and it was intense. He had actually felt something. In that instant that Tommy's eyes met theirs, Tommy had communicated something to them.   It was another feeling, an emotion that Tommy had not expressed before. He thought, "What do the humans call it?"

Sorgo "heard" the Commander's thoughts. *"I think, Commander, the humans call it Love,"* Sorgo offered gently.

"Yes, of course," the Commander said without emotion. He started to turn to leave, but stopped. Then turning toward Sorgo, and looking at her directly, he said, *"Thank you, Sorgo."*

He quickly went out the passageway leaving Tommy with the medical crew.

The Carisians worked furiously throughout the night and the following day to prepare for their departure from Earth Station 3PS-204. Commander Thren had advised the Carisians that the situation with the Earth people was too dangerous to remain. They had discovered their location and were now making efforts to break in using a nuclear device to explode open the Plasma Shield.

* * *

T - minus 3 Hours. Outside.

On the Outside, the "StarBright" teams were working furiously to prepare for the counter-attack on the invaders. The crews were three hours before the detonation. Heavily armed Ranger units with radiation protection gear were standing by to make the initial assault. Another army, this one composed of government scientists, had been flown in to the area and were anxiously waiting for "...the opportunity of a lifetime.

* * *

T - Minus 3 Hours. Earth Station 3PS-204

"Commander Thren, this is Sharma. Mass Accelerator Coupler procedure is completed. Tommy's systems are within normal range. He is asleep and can be moved at any time."

"Thank you, Sharma." The Commander could sense that events were about to overtake both the Carisians and the Earth people. Escape for his crew was the only way to de-fuse this chaotic state.   He sent thought orders, *"Sharma, please prepare Tommy for transport. Arnul, please direct all station crew members to proceed to Corridor 42, Passageway 7 immediately."*

* * *

T-Minus 2 Hours. Outsid

"Captain Mason, this is General Wallace. Do you copy?"

"Yes, sir, Mason here."

"Status and count," the General tersely demanded of the "StarBright" Detonation Team in the ravine.

"All systems operational. At the mark, count stands at T-Minus 2 Hours... Mark!" the Captain called out crisply.

The General then called his Ranger unit. "StarBright" Attack, do you read?"

"Roger.   Ranger Attack unit ready, **sir!**" came the typically enthusiastic reply from the elite airborne unit.

The General nodded his head in silent satisfaction. True, it wasn't the Vietnam, Syria or Afghanistan, but it was a battlefield nonetheless. He turned to his aide and boomed out an order, "Get me a secure line to the White House. I want the Final Fire Order - let's lock and load." He stood up; and he did so his giant frame seemed to loom even larger...and more ominously. He looked out the window of the van that was serving as the Command and Control Center for Operation "StarBright" and said loud enough for everyone to hear but to no one in particular, "Iranian extremists, Taliban insurgents, or aliens from outer space - it's all the same to me." The dusk had turned the surrounding hills to a very dark green, and in the twilight sky, the pale outline of the moon was on the horizon.

For a moment, he thought he saw the twinkle of the first star. Too early in the evening for stars, he thought. He dismissed it.

* * *

T-Minus 2 Hours. Aboard Carisian Intergalactic Explorer

TORLANT   COMMUNICATION: "COMMANDER THREN, THIS IS COMMANDER KRON. WE HAVE DECIDED AGAINST USING A

SHUTTLE CRAFT AND WILL INSTEAD MAKE A FULL APPROACH IN THE EXPLORER. WE HAVE DETECTED HOSTILE EARTH AIRCRAFT WHICH ARE ARMED WITH NUCLEAR MISSILES. THEIR RADIO TRANSMISSIONS INDICATE THAT THEY WOULD USE THEM AGAINST A SHUTTLE CRAFT WHICH, AS YOU KNOW, DOES NOT HAVE PLASMA SHIELDS. WE CONFIRM THE APPROACH VECTORS AND LANDING ZONE COORDINATES. CONVERGENCE WILL BE IN TWO EARTH HOURS."

* * *

T-Minus 2 Hours. Earth Station 3PS-204

TORLANT COMMUNICATION: "THANK YOU, COMMANDER KRON," Thren typed on his monitor. "I ACKNOWLEDGE 2 EARTH HOURS FOR THE CONVERGENCE."

Thren closed the Torlant Communications Network for the last time and sent a thought to Sharma. *"Sharma, is Tommy ready?"*

"Commander, Tommy is still asleep and ready to be transported upon your order; however, I must confess that he is not entirely ready," came Sharma's thought in reply.

Most unlike Sharma, the Commander observed to himself. *"You will please explain upon my arrival to the medical facility."* Without hesitating, the Commander projected a thought to the extreme end of Earth Station 3PS-204, to Corridor 42, Passageway-7.

"Yes, Commander, all members of crew have been accounted for and assembled. Detonation sequence has been coded and countdown to self-destruct has begun," came Arnul's reply slightly delayed by the distance and by the jumble of thoughts by hundreds of Carisians crowded in the outermost corridor.

Commander Thren took one last look around the Control Room. It had been home to him...and now it must be destroyed. For the first time perhaps ever, he allowed himself **to feel**: he felt good about the years he spent here and at the same time, he felt sad to depart. How odd, he thought to himself. Contradictory feelings about the same subject. Earth people live with these contradictory feelings every day of their lives! An amazing race of people. Then he turned and left. Time was running dangerously short.

* * *

T-Minus 1 Hour - Outside

"General Wallace, this is Captain Mason, StarBright Detonation Team."

"Wallace, here, go ahead, Captain.

"At the mark it will be T-minus 1 hour...Mark! I am handing over Final Fire Control to you. Please acknowledge, General."

"This is General Wallace, I acknowledge and am assuming Final Fire Control on my order in T-minus...59 minutes and counting. Captain, you and your men will leave the area to assume your positions in the Green Zone."

"Roger, General. Mason out."

It was now in his hands he thought. In 59 minutes he would push the button, explode the nuclear device and breach the defenses of these hostile aliens. He pictured them in his mind: fangs and horns with saliva dripping, waiting to spawn and then attack the human race...probably, ate that little kid...what was his name? He then called the Ranger Unit for a final check of watches, review orders...and a "look sharp". He signed off and went to the refrigerator to help himself to a diet soda.

* * *

T-Minus 1 Hour. Earth Station 3PS-204

The three Carisians, Thren, Sorgo and Sharma, had formed a close circle around Tommy.

The Commander looked closely at Tommy's placid face. So, this is what he looked like before the accident. Now, the Commander realized how much the boy must have suffered from his injuries. Sharma was right: they could and did correct his physical injuries. The lines and scars on Tommy's face and neck had disappeared. His lips were pink and small; and his nose resembled those of other humans. Here was a young boy with a whole life before him.

"*It was right, Commander, that we helped the boy,*" Sharma offered. "*He would have suffered throughout his life.*"

"*Thank you, Sharma.*" The Commander was truly grateful.

"*Commander Thren, this is Arnul.*" Thren could hardly understand the thoughts. It felt like a loud continuous buzz. The Commander shut his eyes feeling the pain of the noise and trying to "hear" what Arnul was saying.

"*Must leave, immed...time ....last...detonate...several moments,*" was all that the Commander picked up, but it was enough.

They formed an aura around the boy who was still sleeping peacefully on the surgical table. The aura glowed brighter and brighter until it enveloped Tommy, forming a bubble of light. The Carisians stepped back, and slowly, Tommy began to rise off the table as if supported by a cushion of air.

Sorgo sent the thought first, "*Commander, with your permission, I will escort Tommy home.*"

"*Thank you, Sorgo, but that will not be necessary. You will please report to Arnul and assist with the transfer of crew. **I** must take Tommy home.*"

"*As you wish, Commander.*" Sorgo could feel the weight on Thren's shoulders. The Council of the Wise Ones would hold him responsible for this. Turning to look for the last time at her new found friend, she reached her thin delicate hand into the bubble and touched Tommy on the forehead, "*Good-bye, Tommy. I shall...miss you.*" She withdrew her hand and left.

Sharma and the Commander hurried down the maze of corridors with Tommy suspended in the bubble of light between them. They glided rapidly up one corridor and then down another, neither of them offering any thoughts.

After long minutes of a dizzying flight through the corridors, they came to the one the Commander had selected and located the passageway to the Outside. Commander Thren was about to release the locking device which would open the Plasma Shield when he turned to Sharma, "*What did you mean when you said Tommy '...was not entirely ready?'*"

"*Commander, time did not permit the entire memory erasure process to be completed as we had planned. It means that Tommy may remember fragments of his experiences with us; names, perhaps images,*" Sharma replied.

"*I see. Will it cause him pain?*" Thren asked hoping that after all he and they had been through that Tommy would not be hurt any more than he was.

"*No, not pain. Confusion, perhaps. And the frustration which comes from not remembering.*"

"*Thank you, Sharma. You have done well. Now, you must join the others immediately. There are only moments left for you to clear the facility. Commander Kron knows what I am about to do. If I do not return in 60 earth minutes, he will depart.*"

Sharma and the Commander had been together as crewmates for many years. For a moment, Sharma hesitated. He started to offer his help. Surely, between the two of them, they could overcome any difficulties. Thren felt Sharma's thoughts, *"Go, quickly, my friend, Sharma. Please join the others. They will need your assistance,"* the Commander ordered.

"As you wish, Commander." Sharma turned and a moment later had vanished down another corridor.

Instantly, Thren formed a bubble around himself and Tommy. He then released the Plasma Shield. The cold night air rushed in to the facility and within seconds, Earth Station 3PS-204 had been depressurized and contaminated. He drifted out slowly at first from the passageway with Tommy floating on his back alongside him. It would be seconds before the entire earth station would self-destruct and collapse on itself.

They were in the middle of the cornfield, about 2 miles from Tommy's house. Then the Commander started to race across the field, skimming at inches above the ground with Tommy's bubble attached to his own. The ground was a dark blur beneath them. Through the darkness, Thren could see the Flagg's house in the distance off to his right.

The Commander first heard a deep and low "thwump" which sounded almost like a grumble from deep beneath the earth, followed by wave after wave of vibrations that buffeted him, and caused him and Tommy to tumble wildly through the air. He nearly lost the boy as the Kralon bubbles separated for an instant.

The self-destruct mechanism had done its job. Earth Station 3PS-204 would be entombed forever beneath several miles of earth and rock.

The Flagg's felt it too. The porch light went on.

* * *

Zero Hour

General Wallace keyed in the codes for the Final Fire Order as his staff sat along side him at the console. The computer began the countdown sequencing after conducting internal systems checks at each step in the sequence. Finally, with some assistance from his staff, the sequence was completed, and the computer flashed on and off:

FINAL FIRE ORDER: DETONATE.

FINAL FIRE ORDER: DETONATE.

FINAL FIRE ORDER: DETONATE.

They looked apprehensively at each other. They knew he would do it. He had disregarded the Professor's warning about the power of these beings and his plea not to go through with it. Maybe, they were peaceful after all? Maybe, they were just trying to tell us to back off? Maybe, we could have talked? Maybe, we could have.....

It started as a deep and low rumbling beneath them, and then turned into a terrifying, ominous growl from the deep insides of the Earth. Massive waves of vibrations boiled up and spilled over. The van was rocking violently, like a ship being tossed about in a heavy sea. In the van, the General and his staff were also tossed about like little toys being discarded by an angry child. The General threw himself on the computer that was still flashing and awaiting its deadly summons:

FINAL FIRE ORDER: DETONATE.

FINAL FIRE ORDER: DETONATE.

FINAL FIRE ORDER: DETONATE.

The General bellowed, "Why those dirty no good..., they're attacking!"

He started to press the "Enter" key to confirm the detonation order. Everyone took in a breath.

Then...

Nothing.

The lights went out. The computer went out. The telephones went out. The radios stopped. The clocks stopped. Everything ...ceased.

For those outside the van, the night sky was replaced with a blackness that absorbed light from the Moon and the stars. It was as if someone had repainted the sky with black marking ink. Even the air was overtaken by a suffocating darkness. For a few moments, it seemed that everyone might drown in the blackness. There was no sound. There was...nothing.

* * *

Joanna was not quite asleep even though it was well past midnight. Ever since Tommy disappeared, sleep just wouldn't come. Somehow, she could always feel him - out there. It was as if he was just ...just a fingertip away out of reach. But she knew. He **was** out there... somewhere...and, close. Suddenly, she felt a tremor rock her bed. She sat bolt upright. Scott woke up and was tossed out of the bed. The house shook and rattled for several moments as wave after wave of vibrations passed over. And then it stopped.

"What the...what was that?" Scott said rubbing his elbow while sitting on the floor.

"Are you all right?" Joanna asked looking over his side of the bed. "We don't get earthquakes here, do we?"

"Beats me, Joanna." Scott picked himself up, turned on the wall switch for the exterior spot lights and went to the window. Maybe, it was a freak tornado. What he saw instead, made him freeze. His eyes bulged out and his jaw fell open. Joanna heard him draw in his breath and hold it.

"Scott, what's the matter, what is it?" Joanna said rushing over to her husband's side. She looked out the window and saw it too. "Oh, my God, oh my God," was all Joanna could say as she brought both hands to her mouth.

For a few long moments, both Joanna and Scott were like two statues cemented in place.

There, across the road, were two globes of light. Standing in the road was a smallish ...."thing". It looked to Scott like a child wearing a homemade Halloween ghost outfit. Except that it wasn't Halloween. And in the other globe of light was someone lying down floating in the air...and wearing...Tommy's clothes!

"If this is a joke, it's a sick one. If it's not, then someone is going to get hurt," Scott said angrily as he went over to the bedside table for his pistol.

They both went down the stairs and opened the front door.

"Who are you and what do you want?" Scott called out. He knew instinctively that he was not seeing a Halloween costume but they couldn't make out who or what these two creatures were.

The two balls of light crossed over the road to the end of the walkway.

"Don't come any closer, or I'll shoot," Scott called out as he raised the pistol.

Both Joanna and Scott heard a voice, or at least they thought they did. She looked at Scott and he at his wife. Yes, they heard it. They quickly looked at the creature who was standing up with the Halloween outfit. They heard it again.

"I am Commander Thren. I come in peace." He raised his hand in the Carisian sign.

Scott cocked the trigger and was about to fire.

"No, Scott, wait!" Joanna pleaded and held Scott's arm.

"Do not be frightened, Joanna Flagg and Scott Flagg. I will not harm you.". He came closer.

"Don't come any closer, whoever you are. And, how do you know our names." Scott **was** frightened.

"I have come to return your son, Tommy, to you." And with that Thren slowly came forward together with Tommy lying peacefully asleep in the other bubble.

Joanna saw her son floating in a glowing light, and suddenly felt faint. She wanted to speak but couldn't breathe to get the words out. She started to take deep breaths. Scott put his arm around her waist. She wanted to rush forward. She didn't care about the little grayish man, thing, or whatever, standing in front of her. She could see her son, her beloved Tommy. He looked so peaceful in death. At least, now she knew...But, she was interrupted. Not by anyone speaking, but by a voice which seemed to come from inside her head.

"No, Joanna, Tommy is not dead. He's asleep."

"Is that you doing that to me. Your lips aren't moving, but I know you're talking to ...Tommy's not dead? Joanna almost shouted.

"No, Joanna," came the simple reply.

"Then what have you done to him?" Scott said loudly pointing to Tommy, still not convinced of what he was seeing and "hearing".

"We came upon him near our Earth Station. He was seriously injured from the cold. We treated him. And we restored him to his original face before his accident," Thren explained. He then turned and gently floated Tommy over the walkway toward Joanna and Scott much like pushing a bar of soap in a bathtub. As Tommy floated nearer, he said, *"It's quite all right, the bubble of light is to protect him."* As soon as Thren gently settled Tommy into their waiting arms, the light winked out.

Joanna and Scott looked at their son. It was true, it was just as if, it was all a bad dream. His face was...beautiful. Joanna held Tommy's head in her hands and couldn't take her eyes off him. She burst into tears – happy tears. She kissed him, felt his face and kissed him some more. It **was** Tommy! My Tommy is back!

"He will sleep for several more hours. When he awakens, he will only remember the fall in the ravine. We have taken certain measures so that he does not remember us or his stay with us." The Commander was about to turn and go, but then added, *"But we Carisians shall always remember Tommy."*

Joanna was a flood of feelings. She didn't know what to say or feel or do. She didn't know that the little man with the gray skin and the large round eyes was "hearing" her thoughts and trying to feel them as well. She gave Scott the rest of Tommy to hold and slowly went down the steps toward the Commander. As she reached him, she bent over and put her arms around his little neck and gave him a kiss on his smooth gray Carisian cheek.

"Thank you, Commander Thren. Thank you. Thanking you for giving Tommy back to us. God bless you," she said with tears streaming down her cheeks.

Thren slowly reached out and ever so gently touched the tears with his finger and instantly Joanna felt the rush of warmth pour into her. She smiled at him; it was her first smile in so long and it mingled with her tears of joy.

Suddenly, the lights in the night sky disappeared. All the lights in the house went out too. They were enveloped in total silence. Joanna and Scott felt a smothering blackness. There was nothing beyond the reach of their arms. They could barely see the Commander who was only inches away from Joanna.

Thren looked up. His dark eyes seemed to be penetrating this ink black nothingness when a shaft of orange light broke the void. It settled on the other side of the road.

The Commander raised his hand in the Carisian sign of peace and sent a thought, "*Good-bye. May you always have peace.*" Without taking his eyes off the couple and Tommy lying in their arms, he glided backwards across the road and into the shaft of light. He stood in the glow for a few seconds, and raised his hand once more to the Flagg's in a final good-bye. The shaft of light then narrowed to pencil thin, and in an instant retracted into the darkness. Moments later, the blackness disappeared and the night sky sparkled above them.

As they turned to carry him into the house, Tommy stirred in his father's arms. "Sorgo,Glefon, can you....." Then he drifted off to sleep.

EPILOGUE

Everybody had heard about Tommy's sudden return. There were rumors of strange events at the ravine: explosions; earthquake like tremors; something about aliens; a major blackout in the area; and the strangest of all -- Tommy's miraculous recovery.

For weeks after these incidents, the house was constantly surrounded by TV network vans, police and UFO investigators. For weeks after the incident in the ravine, the news coverage was continuous. Newspaper stories entitled "**They are Already Here**;" "**Vanished**;" and "**Aliens Among Us**" brought out a constant flow of people who were curious and fascinated by the fantastic story of an underground civilization of aliens. Friends came by at all hours to congratulate the Flaggs, but the truth was that they all wanted to see if the rumors about Tommy were true. However, within hours after Tommy's return and with the help of Doctor Joe who was the only other person to see Tommy, Joanna and Scott were moved with Tommy to a small fishing village in Vancouver, Canada.

Tommy had questions too. He continued to have dreams, strange dreams. No, they weren't scary, just strange. He would see faces; dark eyes and strange mouths - pursed lips actually - like someone who had just sucked on a lemon. And, then there were the names that came to him in his dreams - always the same names: Sorgo and Glefon. He couldn't put his finger on it. Why those names?   Who are they? And who was the Commander, Sharma? He asked his Mom and Dad about it. "Friends," was always their reply. Strange.

For years, Tommy never stopped dreaming the same dream, seeing the same faces and recalling the same names. As he grew older, he became convinced that there was a lot more to this recurring dream. One chilly night as he sat huddled on the beach listening to waves washing in from the dark ocean ahead of him, he looked up into the night sky and thought, *"Sorgo, Glefon, who are you, really?"*

All of a sudden, he felt a wonderful rush of warmth flood into him and he heard, ...no, not heard but rather thought he heard, *"Hello, Tommy."*

Tommy smiled. And then it all came back to him. He knew.

"Hello, Sorgo; hello, Glefon."

www.ingramcontent.com/pod-product-compliance
Lightning Source LLC
Chambersburg PA
CBHW041049310726
48978CB00011BA/480